BETRAYAL

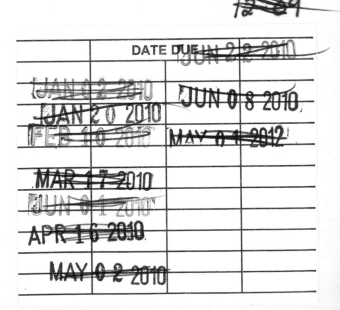

BETRAYAL

DWAYNE S. JOSEPH

www.urbanbooks.net

12 -09
15 —

Urban Books, LLC
1199 Straight Path
West Babylon, NY 11704

Betrayal copyright© 2009 Dwayne S. Joseph

ISBN-13: 978-1-60162-190-0
ISBN-10: 1-60162-190-6

First Trade Printing October 2009
Printed in the United States of America

10 9 8 7 6 5 4 3 2

Distributed by Kensington Publishing Corp.
Submit Wholesale Orders to:
Kensington Publishing Corp.
C/O Penguin Group (USA) Inc.
Attention: Order Processing
405 Murray Hill Parkway
East Rutherford, NJ 07073-2316
Phone: 1-800-526-0275
Fax: 1-800-227-9604

Acknowledgments

Wow! It's done! Finally! I can breathe now. Well, at least for a little. *Betrayal* was work. Started in early '08, and finished in early '09. I've never taken this long to write a book before, but '08 was a crazy, frustrating, hectic, exciting (New York Giants—Super Bowl Champs!), and monumental (Can we say Obama, Obama!) year. For a brief moment in '08, writing stopped being fun, so I put down the pen for a while, but then I finally picked it back up, and when I did, *Betrayal* took off.

If you all follow me, you know I do all I can to step up to my own personal challenge of growth with each book. Once again, I've done that. *Betrayal* is intense, dark, and suspenseful . . . it is one hell of a roller coaster ride and it was a hell of a lot of fun to write! Flip the pages and you'll see, but before you do . . .

God—thanks for the strength to endure life's challenges. Wendy—Thank you for helping inspire and ignite my flame when it starts to go out. Seeing your excitement and enthusiasm for this book was a beautiful thing. I love you! Tatiana, Natalia, and X—OK, Daddy has stopped living at Barnes & Noble . . . at least for now. Thank you kids for never allowing life to be dull. I love you! Ready for a tight? 1, 2, 3 . . . tiiiiiiight! My family—thank you for the support! Keep doing big things, Tre! I love you guys! Granny, Grandmother—my hearts! My friends—much love for all of you! To my Xbox 360 crew: We've grown and I'm still giving out headshots and sawing you in half! Lol!

Thanks to Carl, Martha, Natalie, and the rest of the Urban Books staff. Smiley . . . Hell of a cover, kid!

To the book clubs: Sweet Soul Sisters, One Book @ A Time, The African Violets Book Club, C.A.T.T.S., African American Sisters In Spirit, Sisters In Spirit II, Brown Sugar Sistahs With Books, Page Turnas Book Club, For Da Sista's Book Club, Aminia Book Club, Circle of Women, Ujima Nia, Sister 2 Sister, Ebony Jewells Book Club, Sistahs On The Reading Edge, Cushcity.com, Between The Covers Literary Group, B~More Readers With W.I.S.D.O.M., The Woman In Me 2002 Book Club, Cyrus A Webb & the Conversations Book Club, Nubian Sista's Book Club, Savvy Book Club, The Distinct Ladies Book Club: It has truly been an honor for me to have met or conversed with you all. I cannot thank you enough for the great time and honest feedback that you all provide.

To Elyse Draper, Marlena Hendrickson, Nakea Murray from 3 Chicks On Lit, Dedan Tolbert, Sam Redd (The Maverick), Tangela Williams from APOOO, Eva Leger, Deb, and the rest of the Urbanfirebooks crew, Dana Y. Bowles, Heather Covington from Disilgold, Misty Erickson, Candace Jones (Hanna '92!), Laura Ford, Patricia Ford, Kellie Blizzard, Crystal Williams, Latonya Stewart, Von McIntire, LaVonne Jones, Melinda Mooneyhan, Jessica Robinson, Beatrice Bautista, Mondell T. Pope . . . thank you guys for your support!!

To Wendy, Jeri Wiggins, Portia Cannon (Million thanks and blessings), Nicole Littlejohn, Jocelyn Lawson and Nancy Silvas, Janey Rios . . . I cannot thank you ladies enough for reading and being patient as I kept you in suspense chapter by chapter! I brought it, didn't I!

To the rest of the readers . . . don't stop hitting me up on Myspace, Facebook, iseecolor.com, or my e-mail. Receiving your feedback and messages is an honor!! Keep those reviews coming.

Peron F. Long, Eric Pete, LaJill Hunt, Anna J . . . We still have work to do. Let's continue to stay above!!

To Leigh Leshner and Fred Fontana—Thank you both! Let's make it happen in '09!!!

To Barb, Gideon, and the rest of the crew at the café at the Barnes & Noble in Ellicott City . . . thanks for keeping the vanilla lattes warm, the Mountain Dew on hand, and the oatmeal raisin cookies fresh! I'll be there working on the next book sitting at my table on the left!! Oh . . . and I promise I'll be a Barnes & Noble member this year!

Finally to my G-Men!! We didn't repeat as champs this year, but have no doubt, we are the Beeeest! Big Blue for life! Spags . . . you will be missed. Osi . . . welcome back! Plax . . . man . . . what can I say . . . what you'll be missed too. G-Men for life!!

A'ight, everyone . . . go read and oh yeah . . . watch out for the sequel to *Home Wrecker*. Yeah . . . your girl, Lisette, is coming back!

Much love!
Dwayne S. Joseph
www.myspace.com/Dwaynesjoseph
Djoseph21044@yahoo.com

Chapter 1

"**I** want you to kill my wife."

Ezekiel hadn't expected the words to have flown so freely from his mouth. Smooth. No hesitation. Silk, the way it had come out.

I want you to kill my wife.

He sat back in his chair and watched his son-in-law, Sam, digest the seven fluid words he'd spoken.

I want you to kill my wife.

Air sighed evenly through his nostrils and down to his lungs, where it swirled around momentarily before rising back up and passing out through his nasal passages. For the first time in a week, breathing didn't hurt his chest. For the first time in eleven days, the weight that had been bearing down on his shoulders lessened. It wasn't much, but it was just enough. He wanted his wife killed. Dead. Gone. Extinct. He intertwined his fingers in his lap.

Sam stared at him, his forehead knotted up. Zeke saw

the struggle. The confusion did the jitterbug with disbelief and fear in his eyes.

"You're kidding, right?"

Sam stared at his father-in-law as his father-in-law stared back at him, a chill creeping up from the base of his spine to the back of his neck. Ezekiel had yet to respond, but in his eyes Sam saw an answer that made his throat dry. He cleared it and said again, "Zeke, you're . . . you're kidding, right?"

Zeke looked at Sam and still wouldn't respond. He just stared and read Sam's thoughts through the pleading in his eyes. He wanted him to smile and break out in laughter. He wanted him to say that he was indeed kidding.

Ten days ago, that would have been the case. Ten days ago, the earth hadn't rotated off of its axis yet. The stars hadn't fallen out of the sky. A cow hadn't jumped over the moon. Pigs hadn't yet learned to fly.

Eleven days ago, his world hadn't been turned upside down.

It was a Thursday. It had been cold. The March wind had been brutal and unkind. But it had been sunny and bright, and there had been no snow on the ground.

But then came Friday.

Snow still hadn't fallen, but the sun had been taken hostage by black clouds moving ominously in the sky. The wind was gone, but the air's vicious bite remained.

Zeke said, "Do you know me to kid around, Sam?"

Sam clenched his jaws, squinted his eyes a bit. "You can't be serious."

"I'm very serious, Sam."

Sam shook his head. "Come on, Zeke. This shit's not funny."

"I told you, I'm not making any jokes."

"No way," Sam said, cracking his knuckles. "No way at all that you're not fucking with me."

"Is there a problem?"

"Is there a . . . " Sam paused and shook his head again. "You're talking about killing your wife. Shit, you're talking about me killing your wife. For real . . . Have you lost your fucking mind? Because this shit is crazy, Zeke. The shit coming out of your mouth right now is crazy."

Zeke locked his eyes on Sam's. His back remained flat against the leather of his chair. His breathing remained steady. "I'm not crazy," he said. "And this isn't crazy. This is what it's going to take to keep me from ruining your life."

Sam looked at Zeke intensely, looking for madness in his father-in-law's eyes. He cracked a few more knuckles, cleared his throat, said, "Zeke . . . come on . . ."

Zeke cut him off. "I walked in on you fucking our intern, Sam."

Sam dragged his hand down over his face, leaned forward in the chair he'd been sitting in, and rested his elbows on his knees. "Come on, Zeke. It was a mistake. It didn't mean anything."

"I don't give a shit whether it meant anything or not, Sam. You fucked around on my little girl!"

Sam sat back uncomfortably in the chair. He exhaled. "I . . . I know, and I'm sorry, Zeke. Believe me when I say I regret it."

Zeke flared his nostrils. He could feel the control slipping away. Bruce Banner was threatening to disappear and leave Sam alone with the Incredible Hulk, who wanted nothing more than to reach across the desk, wrap his thick fingers around Sam's throat, and squeeze until Sam, too, was extinct.

Eleven days ago.

A Friday.

Zeke had received an anonymous package at his office.

A manila envelope with photographs of his wife fucking another man.

She was straddled atop her partner, her back to him. The photographer had skill and one hell of a camera. The divine, fulfilled ecstasy plastered on Zeke's wife's face had been captured beautifully. The way she'd bitten down on her bottom lip. The way her eyes had been rolling into the back of her head. The way she'd been grabbing her breasts and squeezing her nipples.

Zeke had always had a voyeuristic nature about him, and had it been anyone else in the photo he would have unzipped his pants, pulled out his dick, and stroked until he exploded all over the expensive photo paper, imagining that his cum were actually being spilled on her breasts, her ass, in her mouth.

But it hadn't been anyone else.

It had been his wife.

And she was enjoying another man's dick.

After looking at the photographs, he threw up whatever food he'd eaten that day. He dry heaved when he had nothing left.

He looked at the pictures again. Maybe his eyes had been playing tricks on him. He had been working longer hours preparing for another opening. Maybe the fatigue had fucked with his head and helped create an image that hadn't been real. The sickest kind of mirage.

He stared at the pictures. Waited for the image to change as he rifled through them. Waited for the image to fade, the way a pool of fresh water in the middle of the desert did when the sun was at its unbearably highest point.

He waited.

And waited.

And waited some more.

Then he gagged, dry heaved again.

Unlike the water that disappeared just before you ate sand, the image of his wife on top of another man had no disappearing act.

Zeke looked over the manila envelope for a name, an address . . . something to let him know who had sent the pictures. He looked at the back of each 8x11 glossed copy.

No name.

No insignia.

No coded message viewable under the light or in the dark.

For hours he sat with the photographs spread out before him, his mind working, wondering, questioning.

Why?

He thought back to the last time they'd made love. Loving words were spoken, tender caresses and gentle kisses given. All had seemed right with the world, despite their sparse sex life. Had that been the reason for his wife's infidelity? Had his hectic work schedule pushed her into another man's arms?

Hours passed. Zeke just sat. Unmoving. Barely breathing. Just staring.

His wife.

The woman he loved more than life itself.

He stared at her long and hard. He would have been staring at the man, too, but his face hadn't been captured in any of the photos. Unless the photographer was the man himself, which Zeke doubted, then the photographer was sending a clear message that the man didn't matter. It could have been any man.

Zeke stared.

At his wife.

At the pleasure in her beautiful face, which had instantaneously become as ugly as sin to him. His temples throbbed with a sharp pain as questions ran through his mind.

Who had sent the pictures?

More importantly—why?

Were they trying to punish him? Punish her? Punish them both?

What was their motive?

Was another package on the way?

Would it be worse?

Hell, could it possibly have been any worse than what he had already received?

It was nearly one in the morning before he slid the photos back into the envelope and then put the envelope in his briefcase and headed home, his head and heart aching. During the entire forty-five minute drive, he kept asking himself what the hell he was going to do when he got home. Would he throw the photos in his wife's face and demand to know who the fuck she'd been riding? Would he threaten her and throw her out of the house? Would he lose it, say to hell with the threat, and just put his hands on her? He didn't know.

He was pissed.

Heartbroken.

Felt damn near homicidal.

He strangled his steering wheel and drove at speeds above ninety miles an hour on the sparse New Jersey Turnpike. Fortunately for him and his wife, he was pulled over by the finest in highway patrol. The twenty-minute delay had given his common sense just enough of a chance to catch up to the rage that had him rocketing toward an OJ Simpson–like home arrival.

Sitting with red and blue flashing lights spiraling behind him, he calmed down enough to rationalize that, first of all, he didn't want to go to jail, and secondly, ending his marriage meant splitting his money with a lying, cheating bitch.

It wasn't easy, but with the $300 ticket thrown beside him, he went home that night and somehow managed to pretend as though he'd never received the anonymous package.

The next day was incredibly difficult for him, as he flip-flopped emotionally throughout the day, going from sadness to hate to rage, and then back to sadness, back to hate, back to rage. Only by staying away from the house for sixteen of the twenty-four hours each day, and then sleeping in his home office for the final eight, had he been able to make it to Sunday. On Sunday, after a hypocritical appearance at church, he went to the office to be alone. Sadness had disappeared; hate and rage were the only emotions coursing through him.

He had to get away. He couldn't handle being close to her. He couldn't look at her anymore. He couldn't take the sound of her voice, the phoniness in it. He couldn't handle the smell of her Victoria Secret perfume, the perfume he'd bought for her. Sunday he avoided committing murder by going to the office to be alone to think.

Thirty-four years.

For how many of them had she been living a lie?

For how many of them had he been played for a fool?

Damn those photos. Damn whoever had sent them.

She'd been his everything. His first, and what would be his last, true love. She had betrayed him. Betrayed his trust. His devotion. Before the photos, he had loved and respected her. After the photos . . . After the photos, love resigned and hate took its place in his heart, beside a small section occupied by a longing ache.

He needed to figure out what his next move would be. They had a life together. They'd raised a daughter. They'd created memories. Memories that he wished he could forget. He had to have her out of his life, because there just was no forgiving her.

But how?

Sunday.

At the office alone.

He'd been hoping for some sort of an answer that day. A way to remain latched on by the fingertips of one hand to the edge of the cliff. That day he found, in Sam's office, the answer he needed to help him grab hold of the cliff with his other hand. Five days later, he was halfway to pulling himself back to salvation. Or losing his sanity. It all depended on which mirror in the spectrum one was looking through.

Chapter 2

"It's too late for regrets, Sam. Too late to turn back the clock."

Sam clenched his jaws. Shook his head. Exhaled heavily through his nostrils. "What the hell happened, man? What the hell did Sapphire do?"

"Does it really matter, Sam?"

"Does it . . . You're talking about murder! Of course it matters."

Zeke shook his head. "The only thing that matters right now, Sam, is your life. The past you've outlived. The name and reputation you've established. Everything you have. That's all that matters right now."

Sam put both of his hands on top of his bald head. He wanted to be cool, calm. He hadn't come outright and said what he'd do, but Sam knew what Zeke was threatening and that gave him a dull ache in his temples. "Shit, Zeke. What the fuck?"

"Your life matters to you, doesn't it, Sam?"

"I . . . I can't, Zeke. I can't kill your wife. I can't kill Sapph."

Zeke frowned. "You're breaking my heart, Sam."

"Zeke . . ."

"You were the son I never had."

"Zeke . . ."

"Ruining your life . . . doing that . . . it hurts me."

"Zeke . . . please, man . . ."

"This is going to break Jewell's heart, too. Once she knows what you've done. She's going to be devastated."

"Zeke . . . man . . . come on."

Zeke sighed. "I hate that I have to be the one to tell her."

"Zeke . . . it was just a mistake. I'm a man. I'm fucking imperfect. Come on. I know you can relate."

"Thirty-four years, Sam. Thirty-four years and I never once stepped out on my marriage. Thirty-four years. Through good times and bad. Through times when frustration and temptation reared their ugly heads. Thirty-four fucking years. I can't relate to you, Sam. I can't relate to being a man that way."

"Zeke, man . . . I was weak, I know. But, I love Jewell. You've gotta believe me. I love her the way you love Sapphire."

"Sapphire is a fucking unfaithful, lying bitch!" Zeke yelled out suddenly, slamming down his fist on his desktop.

The outburst made Sam jump. He tensed up, stared hard at his father-in-law. He'd been in situations where his life had been on the line. He'd had the blade of a knife pressed hard against his throat to the point of drawing blood. Another time, a different blade had penetrated his abdomen. He'd had the barrel of a loaded gun held against his head and chest before. He'd been shot at two other times. Each and every time the reaper stared down at him with a sickly grin, Sam had stared back and dared death to claim him. He'd never been afraid.

Not like he was now.

Zeke stared back at him with eyes colder than death ever could be. Eyes filled with pure hatred. Eyes clouded by extreme pain.

Sapphire was cheating.

Damn.

"I don't care if you do it yourself, or if you have someone else do it, Sam, but if you don't want to go back to the gutter, then you'll do whatever you have to do to make sure my wife dies. Do you understand?" Zeke fell silent for a moment, his chest heaving up and down, and then said, "Do you?"

Sam swallowed dry saliva. "Damn, Zeke . . . I'm sorry, man. I'm sorry this happened to you."

"I didn't ask if you were sorry for me," Zeke said. "I asked if you understood."

Sam wanted to look away, but couldn't. His heart beat heavily. His palms were sweaty, cold. He got the chills. "I . . . I . . ." He paused, unsure of what to say, unsure of what he could say. He'd killed before, but the act had been done under different circumstances.

Zeke studied the conflict in his son-in-law's eyes. It truly hurt him to give the ultimatum, but he had no choice. His wife had betrayed him. Sam had betrayed his daughter.

Betrayal.

They both had to pay.

"How important is your life to you, Sam?"

Sam's shoulders fell, and his chin dropped to his chest. He let out a long exhale. "I . . . I can't make this decision now, Zeke. I . . . I need time."

Zeke flared his nostrils and looked at Sam through narrowed eyes. *They both have to pay*, he thought. "You have two days," he said. "Two days and then I want my answer. Do you understand?"

Sam looked up at his father-in-law, the man who'd shown him what being a man was all about. This was a situation he never imagined he'd have to face. He nodded.

Zeke stood up. "Say hello to my little girl," he said, and then walked past Sam, leaving him alone in his office.

Chapter 3

Ten minutes later, Sam left Zeke's office and headed to his car. Where he was going, he didn't know. He was reeling, still trying to come to grips with the ultimatum he'd been given. His life was being threatened by a man for whom he'd do anything. A man who'd given him one final chance at life.

Twelve years ago.

Sam had been a different person then. A statistic headed toward a long stretch behind bars, or worse. Sam had no respect for life back then. His or anyone else's. He lived each day to survive by whatever means necessary. He had learned to live that way when his mother, a crack addict, kicked him out of their decrepit box of a studio apartment at age fourteen, because she wanted to use the extra money spent on him to support her addiction. Fourteen years old, with only the clothes on his back, Sam became a product of the street. He learned to remain hidden in the shadows by day and thrive at night, a vampire amongst the prostitutes, pimps, drug users, and dealers that would become his family.

Sam did it all. He robbed, he maimed, he sold drugs, he pimped. Always strapped, he grew up an angry, young black man who lived life without fear, remorse, or regret.

Take or get taken out.

That was his mantra. Despite that death's pounding on his door grew louder each day—that was how he lived. That was how he survived.

Take or get taken out.

From fourteen to seventeen, he never got taken. But then he turned eighteen, and his good fortune changed. For the next four years, he was taken far more than he took. Taken to jail, that is. By the time he was twenty-two, the rap sheet he'd amassed had been sadly impressive. Breaking and entering, aggravated assault, drug possession, DUI, car theft. From eighteen to twenty-two, he spent almost more time on lockdown than he did on the streets.

His mother kicked him out to further her habit, from which she eventually passed away, and he'd become another lost soul with his hand on the knob, ready to turn and let death come waltzing inside. That was the man he'd been twelve years ago. No future, but more jail or sure death in sight.

And then he met Zeke.

He'd been walking to his car. A Mercedes. Sam didn't know much about cars back then, but he knew how valuable a Benz was, especially to the owner of the chop shop he used to deal with before his last stay in prison. A Benz, especially one as pristine as the one Zeke had been walking to, would net him a good amount of money. Far more than the dishwashing job his parole officer had him doing.

Tucked away in the dark at the side of a building, Sam

watched Zeke approach the Benz. He was wearing a black suit that looked tailored and expensive. His black leather shoes looked as though they'd been cut from the same cloth of money as the suit. He wore a black fedora on his head, similar to the type Frank Sinatra used to wear, and he had a black trench coat slung over his arm. He was giving off a strong odor, one Sam caught a whiff of instantly: money.

Sam looked down at his Polo sweat suit, an outfit he thought he'd been fronting hard in, and then looked back at Zeke. Money was practically falling from his pockets as he walked without a care. In Zeke, he saw everything that he would never have. Money. A high paying job. An expensive ride to roll around in. A big house with lots of rooms, six or more, with a pool, and a Jacuzzi. A banging-ass wife or girlfriend, or both. Sam scowled, and hate welled instantaneously.

Hate for Zeke.

Hate for his success.

Hate for everything he had.

Hate for Sam's own failures.

Hate for his mother for sending him to a life void of hope.

Hate for a father he never knew.

Hate for his parole officer, although he was probably one of the only people left who may have actually given a shit about him.

Hate for the pimps, prostitutes, drug dealers, and hustlers he called family to that very day.

Hate.

With one more arrest, Sam would go to jail and wouldn't come out for a long while.

Sam thought about leaving Zeke alone and heading

back to the halfway house where he lived, to make it back before curfew passed. He stared hard at Zeke. Sized him up. He was big, but older. Sam surmised that he could take him out. He scowled again, as the voice of reason sat upon his right shoulder and begged him to go home. Sam took a breath. Stared at Zeke. Thunder rumbled in the sky. Sam exhaled. And then he kicked the voice of reason off of his shoulder and moved, thinking that he was only going to go to jail if he got caught.

If.

Hurrying behind Zeke, he was determined to make sure that didn't happen. One blow to the side of his head. Two, if necessary. That would be enough to knock him out and take whatever cash he had, and the keys to the Benz. One unsuspecting blow.

Unfortunately for him, he didn't know that Zeke, a former Marine, had been aware of his presence since he'd first exited the building. He didn't know that Zeke had known something was about to go down. That he could smell it the way he could smell the quickly approaching rainstorm.

Sam never saw it coming. The blow he was supposed to administer was given to him first.

One to his nose, and then another to his midsection, and then finally a sweeping kick, taking his legs from beneath him, sending him crashing hard to the ground. In a matter of seconds, Sam's thoughts of driving away in a Benz with cash in his hands and more on the way quickly disappeared.

Bleeding heavily from his nose, and nauseous from the punch to his stomach, Sam was dazed, confused, and embarrassed. He tried to stand up, but was forced back down by the heel of Zeke's expensive leather shoe.

"I wouldn't get up if I were you."

Sam looked up at Zeke. Spots were flashing in his eyes, the result of the stinging pain from the blows he'd received, particularly the one to his nose. He said, "You broke my fucking nose!"

Zeke said, "Guess you regret trying to approach me now, huh?"

Sam leaned his head back to try to slow the blood flow. "Shit, nigga. Goddamn!"

Zeke reached into the inside pocket of his blazer, removed a handkerchief, and extended it to Sam. "Here. This'll work better than your hand."

Sam looked up at him and said, "Fuck you, nigga. I don't need your shit."

Zeke shook his head, and then reached into the outside pocket of his blazer and pulled out a cell phone. Sam's eyes widened at the sight of it. Zeke said, "I'm willing to bet that you've been arrested before. I'm also willing to bet from the punk-ass look in your eyes that my calling the police would be a very bad thing for you. Am I right?"

Sam winced from the pain in his broken nose, and said, "Fuck you, nigga." He was worried, but had to remain defiant. He'd been punked enough as it was.

Zeke laughed. "Fuck me? OK . . . if that's the way you really want to play it." He flipped the cell open to dial 9-1-1.

"Come on, nigga!" Sam said before Zeke's finger could press the nine. "I'm on the fucking ground with a broken-ass nose. Just get in your shit, nigga, and go."

Zeke stared at Sam and fought back a satisfied smile. The younger generation had no clue what being hard was all about.

He held out the handkerchief again.

This time, Sam took it.

Zeke shook his head disdainfully. "You know, you young guys think you're so damn hard, but you have no clue. You have no idea how easy you have it now. You don't know what struggling really is. You don't know what it's like to have lived during a time when the ceiling was so low, there was only so far you could go. No one had to be politically correct. Affirmative action wasn't in effect. To get anything, to become anything, you had to work hard. You had to be truly hard. Resilient. How old are you?"

The handkerchief catching his blood, Sam said, "What you wanna know for, nigga?"

Zeke closed his eyes a bit, then made a move again to dial 9-1-1.

Sam said, "Twenty-two. Shit!"

"Twenty-two," Zeke repeated with a sigh. "Sad."

"Whatever, nigga."

"Zeke."

"What?"

"My name. Zeke. Not 'nigga.' Call me a nigga again and I'm dialing."

Sam looked at him, and, knowing the older man wasn't playing around, said, "Whatever, man."

"Yeah . . . whatever," Zeke said. "Stand up."

Sam looked at Zeke, his eyes filled with confusion. *Why won't this motherfucker leave or just call the cops and be done with it? Why the hell is he talking to me in a civilized, calm tone? What the fuck does he want me to stand for?*

"Would you rather stay down on the ground?" Zeke said, as if reading his mind.

Sam clenched his jaws and slowly rose to his feet. He wanted to strike out at Zeke, get him back for the sucker punches he didn't get a chance to give earlier. But something told him his efforts would be futile. He stood still with the white handkerchief painted almost completely blood red, and looked at Zeke.

"Are you hungry?" Zeke asked, putting the phone back into his pocket.

Sam knotted up his forehead. "What?"

"I'm going to get something to eat. Are you hungry?"

Sam said, "Are you crazy, ni . . ." He paused, not letting the rest of the word escape.

Zeke shook his head. "I'm just hungry. Now, if you're hungry too, we can get your nose checked out and then get a bite to eat on me. It's up to you."

Sam said, "What the . . . ? Are you looking for some kind of special favor? 'Cause I don't give a fuck . . . that shit ain't happening."

Zeke let out a hard belt of laughter. "Son, I'm a happily married man. I'm definitely not looking for any special favors." He laughed again.

His laughter actually put Sam at ease a little. "A'ight. 'Cause I'm just saying, I'll be dead before that shit goes down."

Zeke chuckled. "No favors needed, son. Now . . . are you hungry or not?"

Thunder rumbled in the sky again. The breeze was picking up, becoming crisp, forceful. The storm was getting closer. Sam looked at Zeke. Something about the older guy gave him a chill, a feeling that if he answered the question correctly his life could possibly be changed forever. He'd had the same sort of life-changing feeling only once before: the day his mother kicked him out. That entire day, something had irked him. Something had pulled at the back of his neck and wouldn't let go. He knew something bad was going to happen that day. The world had just seemed off.

Zeke watched Sam. "I understand your hesitation, you know," he said. "I'm a total stranger, a man you just tried to rob, offering to take you to the E.R. and then to get a bite to eat. If I were in your position, I'd wonder if you were looking for a special favor too. I really should just say 'to hell with it' and call the police." He paused, let his words sink in.

"But honestly, son, I sympathize with what you're going through. I don't know you, or anything about you, but I recognize your struggle. You're desperately searching for the right path. Society has abandoned you and labeled you as just another 'thug nigga.' You're worth nothing and you're going nowhere. You have absolutely nothing to contribute to the world."

Zeke paused again.

Sam watched him. He thought about speaking, but he saw a look in Zeke's eyes—a familiarity in them—that grabbed his attention and caused him to keep his tongue quiet.

Zeke continued, "Believe it or not, I understand what you're feeling inside. I was abandoned. Had a father who'd spent his whole life in jail. A mother who just couldn't stop using heroine. I would have been out on the street like you had I not had an aunt who refused to let me fall through the cracks in life. That's the difference between you and me. I had support—real support. Like I said, I don't know you, but I'm willing to bet you don't have anyone but yourself."

"Now . . . I've never done anything like this before, and hell, maybe I'm crazy for doing so, but for some reason, I feel compelled to do what I know no one else would—especially no one you tried to rob. So . . . are you hungry?"

Sam clenched his jaws. Pain from his nose was shooting through him, but for a moment he didn't feel it. He stared at Zeke. No one had ever taken the time to talk to him this way. No one had ever cared. Zeke had said he was crazy, and maybe he was, but if that were the case then Sam was just as out of his mind, because he nodded and said, "Yeah . . . a li'l bit."

Zeke nodded and said, "OK. What are you in the mood for?"

"I like Kentucky Fried Chicken."

Zeke chuckled and shook his head. "Why don't I just choose the place?"

Sam shrugged. "A'ight."

"By the way," Zeke said, "What's your name?"

"Sam."

Zeke nodded. "Nice to meet you, Sam."

That had been the beginning of the life Sam knew now. The life that was now being threatened by the very person who'd given it to him.

Sam got into his car—a Mercedes-Benz—and started the engine.

Chapter 4

Sam didn't want to go home yet. He couldn't. He had too much on his mind. The vice grip around his temples was enough pressure. He just couldn't deal with going home and looking into Jewell's pretty, hazel eyes. Eyes that had captured him the minute he'd laid his on them.

He'd been no one then.

Just a thug given a one-time opportunity to scratch and claw his way out of the hole he'd dug for himself. A one-time, final chance.

Sam drove for forty-five minutes back to the past from which he'd escaped: his old neighborhood.

Different now, yet still the same. Hopelessness simmered off of the broken-down, abandoned, boarded-up row houses. It radiated in the glow of the bright spotlights posted by the police, allowing them better vision to see illegal activity against which they were ineffective.

On autopilot, Sam drove two more blocks, then made a left, drove another block, made a right, then another quick left, before pulling to a stop in front of a house at the end of the row that in twelve years hadn't changed. He lowered his tinted window and stared at it. Red brick, cracking and turned brown with dirt. Glass in the windows cracked or gone, replaced now by plywood. The metal screen door was bent and was without netting. The door itself, maroon, was cracked in the middle.

He couldn't see inside, but he didn't need to. He knew what it looked like. Three bedrooms—small, one outlet in each room. Two bathrooms—one full, one half. A kitchen, big enough for three people to fit in at one time. A living room with a fireplace that never worked. A basement big enough to house a mini drug operation.

Sam sighed.

At one point in his life, this had been a place he'd called home.

Living with drug dealers, he hung on the stoop by day and sold the weed and crack-cocaine they bagged inside. By night, he was one of a couple who policed the in-house prostitution ring being run.

Sam shook his head.

It had been his reality for a time, but it was still almost hard for him to believe it had been.

"What you lookin' for, nigga?"

Sam turned his focus to the stoop. He saw them sitting there, watching him. Three guys. Their ages he couldn't tell, but he could see that they were young.

"What you lookin' for, nigga?" one of the three asked again. The tallest and thickest one.

Sam looked at him and frowned. "Nothing, man," he said.

The young thug rose from the stoop. "You sure, nigga?" He was strapped. Sam could tell by the way he was standing. Whatever gun he was concealing made him fearless. Made him feel like the motherfucking man.

Sam sighed again, said, "I'm sure," then raised his window and pulled away.

Two days. Two days to make up his mind.

Sam stared at his past in his rear view mirror as he drove away. The young thug was in the middle of the street, staring in his direction.

How important was his life?

He didn't need two days.

He picked up his cell and pressed number two on his speed dial.

Zeke answered. "Do you have an answer?"

Sam looked in his rear view mirror again. Watched his past fade away in the distance.

He didn't want to go back.

He couldn't go back.

He refused to go back.

He said, "I'll do it," and then he ended the call and pressed down on the gas pedal, making sure his past could never catch up to him.

Chapter 5

Zeke put his cell phone down and dropped his chin to his chest. He was going to get what he wanted. His wife was going to be out of his life. For good. He wanted to feel relief. He wanted to feel joy. She'd hurt him. Broken his heart. Shattered his soul.

This was not supposed to happen.

He and Sapphire were different from the rest of their friends. Their foundation had been built with bricks from the ground up. They were strong, and he'd thought their bond was unbreakable. Of course they had their share of issues. Zeke was a workaholic and could be neglectful. He'd also grown colder as the years had gone on. She wasn't independant enough, and demanded too much of his attention. She needed an outlet, something other than shopping. Issues, but surely nothing that could get in the way of thirty-four years worth of marriage.

And then those damn photographs had come.

Tears trailed down from Zeke's weary eyes, ran over his

cheeks, and dripped in silent, rhythmic syncopation from his black-and-white peppered goatee.

This was not supposed to happen. Infidelity was never supposed to happen because their love was never supposed to die.

Zeke clenched his jaws. His heart ached inside his chest, as the slow leak of tears became a heavy stream. He'd broken down before, but he'd still managed to somehow keep it together. But he was losing it now. Sam had agreed to do it. His nightmarish fantasy would soon become reality.

"This wasn't supposed to happen," he said, his chest burning, his throat dry, sore, his head pounding at the sides. "This wasn't supposed to happen. Bitch. You fucking bitch!"

He pounded his fist on the top of his desk, causing a picture frame with a photograph of Sapphire and their daughter, Jewell, to fall face down.

Zeke clenched his jaws harder.

Tried to fight the tears that threatened to steal his sanity.

Sam had agreed to do it.

His wife would be killed.

Pleasure and extreme pain engulfed him.

"Zeke?"

He looked up.

Sapphire. Knocking on the door to his study. Fiddling with the knob.

"Zeke . . . Are you okay?"

Zeke wiped his eyes frantically and then cleared his throat. "I'm fine," he said, but couldn't conceal the attitude and anger thick in his tone.

"Are you sure?"

Violent thoughts ran through Zeke's mind.

He had a bat upstairs beside the bed that he kept for protection. He imagined beating her down with it, smashing it into her over and over again. He also had a loaded .45 in his desk drawer. He trembled as he thought about reaching into the drawer, pulling it out, aiming it at the door, and squeezing the trigger.

Or he could go to the door, open it, clamp his hands over her ears, and slam the back of her head over and over into the wall.

He said again, "I'm fine."

"I heard you shout and then heard a loud bang," Sapphire said.

"Jesus Christ, Sapphire!" Zeke yelled out. "I'm on the phone dealing with an issue. Do you mind if I get it taken care of!"

Sapphire pulled her head back, the vehemence in his voice shocking her. She tried the doorknob again. "Maybe you can get away with that tone with your employees, Zeke, but not with me."

Violent thoughts and images invaded Zeke's mind again. He squeezed his eyes shut. Saw the pictures of Sapphire and her headless lover again, playing like a movie on a reel-to-reel. He gritted his teeth. He opened and closed his fists. He tried to blink the images away. Tried to make Sapphire disappear.

Nothing worked.

The movie continued to play.

She was still on the other side of the door.

He didn't want to apologize. He just wanted to let loose with more venom. He looked at his desk drawer. Used x-ray vision to stare at the .45 inside. He wanted to make the violent images a reality. All he had to do was open the drawer, wrap his fingers around the butt, raise it, aim, and shoot.

He flared his nostrils. Tried to magically blink Sapphire away again. "I'm sorry. I'm just trying to get this situation taken care of."

Sapphire couldn't figure out why, but she had an eerie feeling that his words had meant so much more. She pursed her lips and nodded. *Sick of this shit*, she thought. She let go of the knob and backed away. *So sick of this shit.*

Without responding to Zeke, she walked away and went upstairs to the bedroom. She checked her hair and makeup, slipped into her Dolce & Gabbana Quad Strap Mary Jane pumps, and grabbed her car keys. She took a final glance at herself in the mirror and then, content with what she saw, went to her car. When she closed the door, she made a call on her BlackBerry.

"Hello?"

No beating around the bush, she said, "I'm coming over, Tre."

"I have company."

"Make her leave."

"You know the rules, Sapphire."

"I'll pay double, Tre. Just make her leave." Sapphire sighed. She wouldn't take no for an answer.

Silence responded for a few seconds before Tre said, "OK."

Sapphire smiled. "I'll be there in a half hour."

She ended the call and hit the button for the garage door to go up. As it did, she glanced at the door leading inside. "This is your fault," she said, her voice heavy with regret and sadness. "This is all your fault." She backed out of the garage and drove off.

Zeke heard her leave and was glad. Another few minutes and everything would have been ruined, because violent desire would have become reality.

Sam said he'd do it.

His wife.

Soon to be dead.

He got up and hurried to his car. He wanted to see just where the fuck she was going.

Chapter 6

"You're quiet tonight. Is something wrong?"

Sam fiddled around with green peas on his plate. He did this for a few seconds and then said, "Huh?"

Jewell sighed. "I said you're quiet. What's wrong?"

Sam turned the corners of his mouth downward and shook his head. He was still staring at the peas and the rest of the food he'd barely touched. He didn't look up. "Nothing," he said.

Jewell watched him closely. His silence and lack of attention were out of character. *Did he know?* "Are you sure? Seems like something is bothering you. You've barely spoken two words since you've been home." *Did he tell you?* She stared at him. Studied him. Tried to find the answer.

Sam kept his head down, his eyes focused on his food. He hadn't eaten much and that had Jewell worried.

Sam cleared his throat and nodded. "I'm fine. Just have some things on my mind."

"What kind of things?" Jewell probed. If he knew . . . would he tell her? "What kind of things, babe?" she pressed as Sam remained silent for just a little too long.

Sam exhaled. "Just some work things."

Jewell's eyes widened. "Work? What's wrong? Are things with my father OK?"

Sam looked up.

Jewell looked at him intensely.

"Your father? Why would you ask?"

Jewell's heart began beating heavily. "I don't know. You mentioned work. I just wondered if everything was all right."

"With Zeke?"

"Yes."

Sam looked at her for seconds that seemed like minutes to both of them. *There is something about the look in his eyes . . .* Jewell thought. *Do you know something?*

"Everything's fine with your dad," Sam said, his eyes on her intently. "Why would you ask?"

His sudden focus made Jewell's heart race faster. She shrugged. "It just seems like whatever is bothering you is pretty big. I know how you and my father can bump heads sometimes. I just wondered if it had anything to do with him, that's all."

Sam straightened his back and shook his head. "No. Nothing to do with him," he said.

Jewell nodded. His response didn't seem genuine. "Are you sure?"

Sam let his fork fall heavily to the plate. "Why are you hounding me, Jewell? I answered the questions, didn't I?"

Jewell snapped her head back. "That wasn't necessary, Sam."

"Hounding me was unnecessary."

"I wasn't trying to hound you. I just don't like to see you stressed out, that's all. Now, if my father—"

"Christ, Jewell! I've told you about any issues Zeke and I have had in the past, haven't I?"

Jewell couldn't deny that. "Yes, but—"

"Then why wouldn't I now?"

Jewell wanted to put up a fight and say something more, but she couldn't. "I don't know."

Sam pushed his chair away from the cherry dining table. "I'm gonna go to the gym for a bit." He stood up.

"Sam?" Jewell said, glaring up at him. "What the hell is wrong with you?"

Sam clenched his jaws and stood still for a moment before looking down at her. "Look . . . I'm sorry for going off like that. I've just got some personnel issues going on with some people—friends—I brought in to the company. I have some tough decisions to make and it's wearing me down right now."

Jewell's glare softened. *He doesn't know.* She said, "I'm sorry to hear that. Is there anything I can do to help?"

Sam shook his head. "No. But thanks for asking."

Jewell smiled. "Anytime. But if you need to talk at all . . . I'm here."

Sam gave her a smile. "I know, baby. That's why I love you."

"And I love you," she replied.

"I'm gonna go. I'll be back in about an hour and a half."

Jewell nodded. "OK."

Sam turned and walked out of the dining room. There'd been no kiss good-bye.

Jewell sighed. For a moment, she'd thought he knew, but sitting alone now she realized that she should have known better. Her father was a private man. He wouldn't tell anyone about the photographs she'd sent to him.

Her mother was having an affair.

She thought about the night she'd found out. She was supposed to have been out with her friend, Von, at a club. Sam was out of town on business. Whenever he went away, Jewell got together with her girlfriend from college. They'd have dinner and then go out for drinks and dancing. Jewell's purpose for going out was never to look for trouble. She just didn't like being home alone. She never had.

She was sitting at a table in the back of a Japanese restaurant against the wall waiting for Von to arrive, when Von called her to cancel. She'd been on her way when her babysitter, Gina, called to let her know that her son, Colin, had thrown up and had developed a sudden fever. Von apologized (of course, Jewell told her there was no need), and headed back home.

Disappointed, Jewell finished the rest of her Cosmopolitan, and stood up to leave. That's when she saw her mother walk into the restaurant with a man who wasn't her father.

Sapphire, oblivious to her daughter's presence, laughed and flirted with the man as they headed to a table near the middle of the crowded restaurant. Jewell sat down quickly, grabbed a menu, and held it in front of her face, watching inconspicuously as her mother carried on as though she weren't a married woman.

Jewell seethed. Her father was busting his ass to continue to provide nothing but the good life—the only life Jewell had ever known. How dare her mother disrespect him this way! And who the hell was her date? He was younger—late twenties. Jewell didn't recognize him from anywhere. How did he know her mother?

Jewell strangled the menu and watched silently, her concentration broken only when the waiter came back to her table and asked if she wanted anything else. She ordered a Coke and then put her focus back on her mother. It was hard, but she fought the desire to confront her, maybe even smack her, and made it through the entire dinner. Her relationship with her mother was already a strained one. It had been since Jewell had been a teenager. This wouldn't help.

An hour and a half later, Sapphire gave her date a sensuous kiss with a lot of tongue, snaked her hand to his crotch, then grabbed her purse and walked out of the restaurant, leaving him there alone. Jewell let five minutes pass before she walked to his table, sat down, and said, "Do you know she's married?"

The man looked at her. "Excuse me?"

Jewell pointed toward the restaurant's doors, her eyes still on him. "That woman who was almost fucking you with her goodbye kiss . . . Do you know she's married?"

"Do I know you?"

Jewell twisted her lips into a sneer. "Practically."

The man's forehead knotted up in confusion. "What do you mean by that?"

"Just answer the question. Do you know she's a married woman?"

The man looked around to see if anyone had been paying attention to their conversation. "Look . . . I don't know who you are, but I think you need to get up and leave."

"That woman is my mother," Jewell snapped in a "now-what" tone.

He looked at her, his eyes narrowing a bit. He was silent for a moment before he said, "Your mother?"

Jewell scowled. "Yes."

"Your mother?" he said again.

Jewell nodded.

He sat back in his chair, raised his eyebrows, and chuckled.

"I don't see anything funny about this," Jewell said, put off by his apparent amusement over the situation.

"Shouldn't you be going off on your mother instead of me?"

"I'm not going off. I just asked you a simple question."

"And I've given you a simple answer."

Jewell closed her eyes a bit. He was arrogant and it pissed her off. "How do you know her?" she asked.

"Don't you think you should be discussing that with her?"

Jewell exhaled. "Look . . . just answer the damn question."

"Nice manners."

"How the hell do you know her?" Jewell asked again, the anger within her building. How the hell could Sapphire cheat on her father? After everything he'd done. The hours and hard work put in. Bitch!

The man folded his arms across his chest. "Don't you think a little civility would help?"

Jewell exhaled and pursed her lips. He was right and she knew it. She needed to change her tone if she wanted answers. She sighed. Relaxed her shoulders a little. Well, at least tried to. She was still tense, tight. She said, "Look . . . I realize you're not the one I need to blame for what I saw. You're just a man doing what men do."

He raised an eyebrow at her comment.

"Just tell me how you know her and I'll leave you alone."

The man watched her for a moment, then said, "So, basically, either I tell you, or you'll continue to harass the hell out of me, right?"

"Pretty much."

He frowned. "Look, I don't know why you didn't just confront your mother, although I'm happy you didn't because that spared me from being in the middle of an ugly situation, but seriously . . . I can't answer your question."

"Why not?"

"Because it would be wrong of me to discuss that with you."

Jewell closed her eyes a bit. "And there's nothing wrong with running around with a married woman?"

The stranger shook his head. "I'm not running around with her."

"Really?" Jewell asked in an you've-got-to-be-kidding-me tone. "Because I would consider having dinner in a restaurant with a married woman running around."

"We were just having a simple dinner."

"Do dinners with married women always end with a tongue going down the throat? Because if that's how a simple dinner is supposed to end, then I've been doing them all wrong."

The man clenched his jaws. "Look—"

"No, you look. I don't know who you are, and I don't particularly care to know who you are. As a matter of fact, I don't even want to know how you met her. Just tell me this . . . do you love her?"

The man unfolded his arms and reached for a glass of

water in front of him. He took a sip and stared at Jewell, but didn't say anything as his line of vision went up and down over her.

Jewell cleared her throat and changed positions slightly. She felt uncomfortable under his gaze, yet at the same time, she felt warm. It had been about a month since she and Sam had been intimate. He'd been distant and inattentive. She knew he had a lot on his mind with work, so she didn't pressure him. But she was horny.

She said, "So?"

"So."

"Are you in love with her?"

The man smiled, and shook his head. "Concerning the relationship I have with your mother, love isn't a requirement."

Jewell looked at him curiously. *"Relationship* you have with her? What's that supposed to mean? What kind of relationship do you have with her?"

He sighed, then reached into his pocket and removed his wallet. "We have one of convenience."

Jewell said, "What are you . . . fuck buddies?"

He removed several twenties and laid them on the table. "Let's just say when she needs me, I'm there."

"When she needs you? So what . . . you're, like, on-call for her?"

"Something like that."

Jewell's mouth hung open as she looked at him. Good-looking, fit, dressed in casual but expensive clothing. *No way*, she thought. She shook her head. "Does . . ." She paused, not believing what she was about to ask. "Does she pay you for your . . . your time?"

He looked at her, and, after a few seconds of silence, said, "Yes."

Jewell got the chills. "Are you . . . a professional?" Her voice dipped as the word escaped from her lips.

The man nodded.

Jewell felt her stomach turn.

Her mother.

Paying for sex.

Using her father's money.

She reached across the table and slapped her mother's gigolo hard across his cheek. "Fuck you!"

The gigolo put his hand to his cheek and said, "My fee is pretty steep."

Jewell said again, "Fuck you."

He shrugged his shoulders. "Just being upfront with you."

Jewell shook her head. She was in shock and disgusted.

Her mother.

Paying for sex.

Using her father's money.

The thoughts ran through her mind over and over.

Her stomach turned.

She got up and walked out of the restaurant. She had to get away. She needed air.

Her mother.

Paying for sex.

Using her father's money.

She made a left out of the restaurant and headed toward her car. She retched, and paused in the parking lot, thinking she was about to throw up. Her mother was paying a gigolo for his time. She looked back toward the restaurant to see her mother's gigolo walking out and heading in the opposite direction.

Bitch, Jewell thought, staring at his back as he sauntered away. He'd left her father's money on the table. He had her father's money in his pocket. Money that her mother had given him. Jewell grit her teeth and closed her fists tightly. *Bitch*, she thought again. She was using her father's hard-earned money to get off. It was selfish and foul.

She thought about a girlfriend of hers who'd found out her husband had been having an affair. To get both the husband and his mistress, who also happened to be married, Jewell's girlfriend had done something very devious and effective. Something that Jewell never imagined she'd be in a position to do.

"I'm not going to let you get away with this," she whispered, and then called out, "Hey!" and took off after her mother's gigolo.

The gigolo turned around.

Jewell stopped just in front of him and said, "She . . . she pays you." It was a statement, not a question.

He nodded. "She does."

"I . . . I want proof." She was on autopilot, speaking without thinking.

"Proof?"

"When you sleep with her . . . do you do it at your place or a hotel?"

"My place. Why?"

Jewell nodded. "Just curious. Anyway . . . I want pictures."

"Pictures? Pictures of what?"

"Of you two having sex."

He smiled. "You're funny."

She didn't smile. "I'm not cracking a joke. I want pictures of you with her."

He shook his head. "You must be delusional if you think I'm going to provide you with snapshots."

Jewell said, "I'll pay you."

"Pay me?"

"Yes. Five thousand dollars. And you won't be in the picture."

"And how would I not be?"

"The person who would take the photo would be a professional. You wouldn't be in the picture."

"Five thousand dollars?"

"Yes."

"Just to capture your mother having sex with me?"

"Not with you. You don't exist. The man in the photo would be just another man."

"You have a pretty sharp mind to come up with something that quick."

Jewell thought about her friend again and said, "I know someone who's done this sort of thing before."

He nodded and said, "So you want to pay me to let a photographer take pictures. Don't you think your mother would have a problem with him being there?"

"I assume you have closets in your bedroom."

"I do."

"Does she go in them?"

"No."

"Then she wouldn't know."

He looked at Jewell.

Jewell looked at him.

Tre closed his eyes a bit. "How do I know for sure that you won't put me in the picture? Or that you won't go putting my business out in the street?"

Her tone no-nonsense, Jewell said, "This is about my mother. Not you. You're just a male whore. You're not important, therefore, you don't need to be in the picture. Trust me . . . your highly *respectable* occupation is safe."

"Make it ten and we have a deal."

"Ten? No way."

He shrugged. "I'm not the one who needs my services."

"Your services? Don't put me in the same category as one of your clients."

"I have what you want and need. What makes you different?"

"I'm not looking for sex."

"Not all of my clients do. Some just want my time. And isn't that what you're looking for?"

Jewell opened her mouth to reply, but then closed it. She wanted to rebut what he was saying, but she couldn't.

"Look . . . why don't you take some time to think about it. Your mother knows how to find me if you want to get in touch with me." He turned to leave.

Jewell shook her head. He'd been right. She did want his time. Maybe not the same type as his other clients, but it was his time nonetheless. She said, "OK."

He turned around. "OK?"

"I'll pay you seven."

He thought about it for a moment and then said, "Deal. But I want it all up front. In cash. Two days from now."

Jewell stared at him. *Asshole*, she thought. She wanted to tell him to go to hell, but she couldn't. Her father had always done whatever he'd had to do to protect her. She was his little princess. Jewell knew he'd put her life before his. She was going to break his heart. She knew that. But just as he'd do anything to for her, she was willing to do the same. She said, "Fine."

Eight days later, she had three sets of photographs that she could barely look at. She sent out two sets the next day.

"I'm sorry, Daddy," she whispered as tears welled in her eyes. "But you had to know."

Chapter 7

"Mmmm. Oh . . . oh, Tre . . . just like that. Yes! Just . . . just like that!"

Sapphire moaned and arched her back to swallow Tre deeper inside of her. She'd already had one orgasm. Another would be coming soon. And another one after that. As she'd been told, the man was gifted. Not only was he fantastically equipped, but he knew how to use his tool with precision.

Sapphire moaned again. Bit down on her bottom lip. Felt chills creep from the base of her spine, up her back, and over her arms. She took in a breath as he pulled her down and thrust upwards. It hurt so good he was so deep. She tightened her walls around his shaft.

Tre clenched his jaws.

He loved when they did that.

He thrust harder, deeper.

Sapphire moaned louder. Said, "Oh God! Oh . . . God, Tre!"

She leaned forward. Gripped his headboard with Japanese writing.

The headboard was a new addition to the décor in his condo. He'd found it online and had it shipped to him from overseas. He was heavy into Japanese culture and style. It was something he'd acquired an appreciation for during his stay in Japan when he'd been a communications specialist for the Air Force. He'd been told by countless fellow airmen how beautiful Japan was and how the women there were without equal.

How right they'd been.

He'd grown up in the callous, gritty, and oftentimes hopeless environment of the inner-city. After spending much of his youth heading aimlessly down the wrong path, he decided from watching a commercial on TV to join the Air Force. He needed direction, and, for some particular reason, the commercial, which he'd seen countless times before, spoke to him. He joined that day, and two weeks later he was off to boot camp. One year after that, he was living in Japan, having the time of his life.

The Japanese culture was so unlike anything he'd ever experienced. The respect the Japanese had for themselves, others, and the land in which they lived connected with him. Within nine months, he was speaking the language almost fluently. Instead of feeling like an outsider, Tre felt more at home there than in his own hood. The men never gave him problems, and the women . . .

To say they loved him would be an understatement.

They couldn't get enough of his mahogany-colored skin. They treated him like royalty, catering to his every need, often before he even realized what his own need was. The women were demure and submissive, but he never took advantage of them the way some of his fellow airmen had.

Even though they never asked for or demanded it, Tre treated them with the same level of respect that he received, and this was one of the main reasons he was so loved.

He'd never had a problem pleasuring women, but in Japan, he honed his skills as though pleasing the opposite sex were an alternate form of jujutsu. Kissing, licking, sucking, nibbling, caressing, massaging, fucking . . . he took it all to another level.

He lived the Japanese lifestyle for three years, and when he came back home to the States, it was impossible to let the culture go, as it had become a part of him. His condo was meticulously decorated in a Japanese décor, and he ate only Japanese cuisine. He even listened to Japanese music, although his preference was still soul from the fifties, sixties, and seventies.

He'd met Sapphire at a Barnes & Noble bookstore. He'd been watching her for twenty minutes. From the moment he'd laid eyes on her, he could tell she was a potential. Her body language had given it away. She was a proud woman, but her posture sagged with depression and unhappiness. Unfulfilled and neglected; he knew those types of women very well. He'd learned to spot them during his time in Japan. Many of the women there had been abandoned souls as their husbands had either been complete workaholics who never made time, or were cheaters giving their time to someone else. Tre learned how to prey on unhappy women by giving them what they yearned for: attention.

Some men strayed in relationships because no matter how good the pussy was at home, they just couldn't be satisfied. Others strayed because their wives had lost interest in sex. Women strayed also. Most tended to because they were no longer being emotionally or physically stimulated at home. Their husband's lack of attention often pushed them into the arms of another man. There were wives, however, who were just like the men whose needs just couldn't be satiated.

Even if it was only temporarily, women needed to feel as though they were all that mattered. Tre understood this. He also understood that women, whether they wanted to admit it or not, when ignored for too long, were willing to pay for a false sense of romance, however temporary it was. There was an overabundance of women in Japan who needed to feel a connection to someone, albeit fleeting. During his stay there, he provided what they needed and did very well for himself. When it was time to come back to the States, he didn't doubt he would do just as well, if not better. And he had.

He'd been in the bookstore looking for his favorite author's new book when Sapphire walked past him. One look was all it had taken for him to forego the book and follow her to the relationship section where she picked up a book that, Tre knew, would never help her save her marriage. From there she went to the café. Tre waited for her to sit down and get comfortable before he approached her, and soon after added her to his clientele list.

Now, Sapphire called out his name and tightened her grip around his headboard. "Give it to me, Tre. Harder! Hurt me! I . . . I paid good money. Fuck me! Show me it's worth it!"

Tre grabbed the sides of her hips tightly and drove his dick deeper into her. As he did, he looked over her shoulder to his closet. Weeks ago, a man had been inside of the closet. A professional photographer hired by Sapphire's own daughter to capture her infidelity. What the photographer had been paid, Tre had no idea, but he'd been paid seven thousand dollars to allow him into his space.

"Take me there, Tre. Ooooh . . . take . . . me . . . there!"

Tre pushed her up and then pulled her back down, his eyes still on his closet door. He was fucking Sapphire as he'd been paid to do, but he wasn't really there. He was back in his favorite Japanese restaurant sitting across from Sapphire's daughter.

She'd approached him and gone off with rapid fire questions about whether he'd known Sapphire had been married, before revealing that she was Sapphire's daughter. The revelation had caught him by surprise. Of all of the scenarios he'd imagined possibly getting into in his line of work as a professional gigolo, that was certainly one scenario he'd never thought of. Of course, it wouldn't have happened had he not gone against his own protocol that night.

His relationship with Sapphire was purely a sexual one. When she wanted or needed to get off, he would be there to satisfy and collect. That night, however, she'd begged for more of his time. Tre had pushed back initially, but when she offered to pay an additional two thousand, he acquiesced and agreed to take her out on a faux date.

He couldn't help but laugh when Sapphire's twin made her identity known. Same eyes. Same nose, though a little wider. Same lips, but thicker, more sensuous. Without question, she was Sapphire's twin, only younger and much sexier.

He'd looked her over, admiring the cleavage that showed in the silk blouse she had on. He'd surmised that she was a C-cup, and wondered if her nipples were large or small, and whether they became erect when they were pinched, licked, or sucked the way Sapphire's did. He thought about palming and sucking on them. Imagined what they would look like as they bounced up and down.

His eyes had trailed down momentarily, and even though the table was covering the bottom half of her, wondered if her pussy was shaved like her mother's. Wondered if it was as tight or got as wet. He stared until she'd cleared her throat and shifted her position.

As surprising as the predicament was, it amused him even more.

Of course, she hadn't found anything funny and proceeded to ramble on with questions about his relationship with her mother. Questions to which he provided answers. Something he felt compelled to do, although he didn't know why.

After answering questions he shouldn't have answered and giving information he shouldn't have given, she stormed out of the restaurant. He left seconds later, chuckling to himself. He was on his way home when she chased him with a proposition that he couldn't turn down.

"Oh Tre!" Sapphire cried, "I need this so bad. Give it to me! Give . . . it . . . to . . . me!"

Tre drove his dick deeper as he continued to stare at his empty closet.

A week after his confrontation with Sapphire's daughter, he fucked Sapphire while the professional photographer took flashless photographs. Two days after the photos were taken, he received a set in the mail. His head had been cut off in each picture.

He thrust upward again.

Made Sapphire gasp, moan. Made her say, "Oh my God!"

He looked away from the closet and looked up at her.

Her eyes were closed tightly. She was lost in the sex, oblivious to his lack of interest.

He thrust into her again. Hard.

She paid well to be fucked well, and when it came to money, Tre always delivered.

Chapter 8

One hour later, Sapphire walked out of Tre's condominium complex. She was starving. Starving and exhausted. Tre had put it on her good. He was well worth the money she'd paid.

She tightened the belt of her leather coat. The October wind was biting. It was going to be a cold winter. She could feel it. She shivered and felt her body yawn. She was going to sleep hard when she got home. But first she needed to put back the calories she'd burned off in Tre's bed.

Japanese.

The décor in Tre's condo had given her a craving for it. Two blocks from where she'd parked was an excellent Japanese restaurant Tre had taken her to once before. She would hit the restaurant and then head back to her car and go home. She shivered again as the wind blew. She should have been cold, but despite the quiver, she wasn't. She was still hot. Still burning from the sex.

Incredible sex.

Sex she couldn't get enough of.

Sex she paid for.

She shook her head. Her association with Tre had been going on for six months now. She still found it hard to believe that she had any association with him at all.

She'd met Tre by chance at a Barnes & Noble. She'd been sitting in the café, sipping a cappuccino and reading a novel on relationships when Tre approached her.

"You know . . . that book won't help."

Sapphire looked up. "Excuse me?"

Tre pointed to the book. "You can read that two times and others like it, but it's not going to make him pay any more attention to you."

Sapphire stared at him. *What does he know?* she wondered. For some reason, something in his eyes told her that he knew a lot.

She said, "Sorry, but I'm reading this for a friend."

Tre smiled. It was bad-boy handsome and made bumps rise on Sapphire's arms.

He sat down across from her and said, "You're beautiful, sexy, sophisticated, and engaging. He's not stupid enough to cheat on you. He's a workaholic. Spends every hour he can working. You eat dinner alone because he's never there. You haven't had a real vacation in maybe over a year. You and your husband used to be close, but now you're like roommates or, at times, strangers. There's no intimacy. You miss that. You miss being touched. You miss being kissed, caressed, and fondled. You miss making love. You miss being fucked."

He paused to ensure that his last statement made an impact. He stared at her intently. She stared back, speechless. She'd felt every word.

Tre continued, "You're flipping through those pages

hoping that this book will be the one to help you save your marriage, because you can't go on much longer. The depression and loneliness is becoming too much for you to bear."

Tre stopped talking again and looked at her. Quiet shock spread across her face. He'd described her to a T.

Sapphire wanted to respond to him, but didn't know what to say. She shifted in her seat and cleared her throat. She tried to find the right words, but remained silent. In a matter of seconds, this stranger had taken down her wall and left her completely naked. She cleared her throat again. She tried to keep it from happening, but couldn't; her eyes welled with tears. She was emotionally beaten.

His words.

So true.

Tears fell from the corners of her eyes.

Tre said, "I know a lot of women like you. Too many."

Sapphire dabbed at her eyes with a napkin. "Are you a therapist?"

Tre shook his head. "Aspirin."

"Aspirin? What does that mean?"

"Means I can't cure what's ailing you, but I can provide relief."

Sapphire looked at him curiously. "I'm not sure I understand what you mean."

Tre looked at her. Then looked at the ring on her finger. He reached into the breast pocket of his blazer and pulled out a card. He held it out for Sapphire.

She took it and looked it over. Black on both sides, with his name and number in gold on one side.

"I can temporarily satisfy you. All you have to do is call me." He stood up. "It was a pleasure," he said, and then turned and walked off.

Sapphire looked at the card and then at him as he walked out of the bookstore. She looked down at the card again. He was offering his services. She should have been angry, offended that he would even approach her, but for some reason, she wasn't.

There'd been something about him. Something intriguing. Something true.

He'd offered temporary satisfaction.

It should have repulsed her, but the fact of the matter was the offer seemed to call out to her.

Temporary satisfaction.

He was right. The depression and loneliness had been too much to bear.

She slid the card into her purse and left the table, leaving the book there face down. She endured loneliness for two more months before she eventually called Tre.

Now, Sapphire sighed. She had felt guilt initially for going to Tre, but the more Zeke ignored her, the more Tre's temporary satisfaction became a necessity.

Now she was addicted.

The wind blew.

She felt a gush between her legs.

She'd be calling Tre again. Soon.

She went to get her Japanese cuisine.

Chapter 9

Sitting in his car across the street, Zeke watched Sapphire as she walked off in the opposite direction of her car. She moved from the sidewalk to the edge of the curb at the end of the block to cross the busy street.

Zeke's fingers tightened around his steering wheel. He wanted to pull out of his space, gun the engine, and meet his wife in the middle of the street. He wanted to feel the impact of his car barreling into her body at ninety miles an hour. He wanted to hear her bones break, see her catapult into the air, and then he wanted to watch her lifeless body fade away in his rear view mirror as he sped off.

He closed his eyes.

Imagined the moment.

Thought about the second before impact.

Sapphire would see him through the glass. She would see the look in his eyes. The hatred he felt for her. He would see the fear, shock, and, just before he took her life, the regret in hers. In that moment, she would regret ever having betrayed him. In that moment, she would ask for forgiveness.

That moment.

Zeke could see it.

He could hear it.

He could feel it.

He breathed in and out slowly. He savored the twisted, deranged image his heart's desire conjured up in his mind.

He breathed.

In.

Out.

Deep breaths.

In.

Out.

His fingers flexed and closed around the steering wheel even more. It groaned beneath his grasp. Zeke took another breath and held it in as though he were taking a toke, and then released it seconds later slowly through his nostrils.

He opened his eyes and looked in Sapphire's direction. She was crossing the street now. Almost halfway. Zeke strangled the steering wheel again, while the homicidal thoughts played in slow motion.

All he had to do was pull out and press down on the gas pedal.

He was no killer, but he wanted to be.

Right then.

Right there.

All he had to do . . .

He sighed as Sapphire made it safely to the other side and kept going. Zeke clenched his jaws. She'd be back for her car. He'd wait. Maybe he'd be ready to cross over to the dark side when she did.

He looked away from her and looked up at the building she'd come out of. He didn't know of any of her friends living there. Was this where the headless man lived? The headless man who'd made his wife cum . . . was he up there? Was this is home? Zeke grabbed his iPhone, found Sapphire's name, and touched the screen to connect the call.

"Zeke?"

He heard the surprise and apprehension in her voice. She was shaken. He said, "Where are you?"

A second of silence passed before she said, "I . . . I'm just getting to Marlene's house."

Zeke gritted his teeth. *Lying bitch.* He knew Marlene didn't live there. "Marlene's? Is everything all right?"

"She's . . . having some issues with her ex. She just wants to talk."

"You never told me you were going anywhere."

"You were on the phone dealing with your situation. I didn't want to bother you anymore. I'm surprised to hear from you. I didn't think you'd notice my being gone."

"I had to go back to the office to take care of some things. I didn't see your car when I left."

"Oh . . . OK. Is everything OK?"

"It will be soon," Zeke answered.

"That's good."

"How long before you get home?"

"I'm not sure. Marlene sounded pretty upset. I think she really wants to vent. Hopefully I won't be too long because I'm tired. How long do you think you'll be?"

"I don't know."

"Do you want me to wait up?"

"No."

"OK."

"Tell Marlene I said hello."

"I will."

Zeke ended the call without saying good-bye, and slammed his phone down on the seat beside him.

Lying bitch.

His mind went to the past as his blood boiled. He thought back to the days when money had been tight, but the good times had been plentiful. He and Sapphire were different people then. Things that mattered actually meant something. Family, friends, time together—they were all savored. Through good times and bad, they had one another and they could rely on the notion that together was going to be forever, because they were meant to be that way.

Bitch.

Zeke sat still, his fingers clamped down hard around the steering wheel, looking up at the building. He was up there. Somewhere. With his wife's scent on him.

Zeke's head throbbed.

His heart ached.

He looked away from the building to see Sapphire walking toward him. She was on the same side of the street, about forty feet away. He watched her through his windshield and steeled himself for a confrontation; surely she had seen him sitting there.

Thirty-five feet away now, Sapphire walked with purpose in her step. It was dark, but Zeke could see the seriousness in her eyes. Eyes he used to stare into and think how fortunate he was to be able to call a woman as beautiful as she, his wife.

Twenty-five feet.

Sam had said he'd do it, but he wouldn't get that chance now, because Zeke would do it himself.

He took a breath, held it, and tried to get himself centered. He'd imagined getting into it with Sapphire so many times since receiving the photographs. He'd screamed and cursed as different scenarios ran over and over in his mind. He was certain one of those scenarios were about to play out in real life, word for word right then and there. He breathed and watched his wife walk toward him.

His wife.

He loathed, hated, and despised her.

He watched her, twenty feet away now, and felt his heart break into pieces.

His wife.

Below the surface of the hate, something burned. He didn't want to feel it. He tried to ignore the rising temperature. He shook his head. Clenched his jaws.

The burning wouldn't go away.

He began to breathe heavily. Hard, quick gasps. He clenched down harder. Felt as though he would shatter his teeth, he was clenching so hard. He knew what the burning was. He tried to make it stop. Tried to make it go away again.

But he couldn't.

As hard as he tried, as hard as he fought against it, the burning couldn't be soothed, because the burning wasn't truly that at all, but something much worse. Something that he pleaded with himself to not feel.

He shook his head again and stared at his wife, who, instead of coming straight to the car, turned and hurried across the busy street, and went back into the building.

Zeke looked at the building's entrance as his heart pounded in his chest. She hadn't seen him. He looked at the entrance and contemplated running after her. His hands were shaking. He had been so sure the confrontation was going to happen.

He gripped his steering wheel again and took several deep breaths. By now she would have reached whatever apartment she was going to. To find her, Zeke would have to go floor by floor, door to door.

He choked the steering wheel and thought about doing just that. But he wouldn't get far. After kicking the first door down, someone would surely call the police. He opened and closed his fingers, causing the leather of the wheel to groan again. He looked at the building for several long seconds and imagined himself barreling in and kicking down doors, kicking ass if he had to.

His wife was in there.

Somewhere.

With the headless man.

He clenched down again. Flared his nostrils and shook his head. She'd betrayed him. He hated her so much, yet at the same time, he still loved her, and admitting and accepting that was painful.

He started the engine and pulled off slowly, as love burned beneath the pain.

Chapter 10

Slowly. Controlled. To the chest.

Now . . . exhale. Push it up. Don't think about the burn.

Back down now. Controlled. Slowly. Inhale. To the middle of the chest. Down. Down.

Now.

Exhale. Push.

All the way up. Don't lock the arms. It has to come back down again.

Sam did three more reps on the bench press and then set the bar down. He lay motionless on the bench, staring up at a stain in the ceiling tile above him, and breathed in and out slowly. He'd pressed two hundred and fifty pounds. It was the most he'd ever done without a spotter.

He took a slow, deep breath, held it, and then let it out slowly. He'd been at the gym for over an hour, but unlike when he usually came to work out, the gym was empty. Save for the Top Forty eighties' music playing from the speakers above, it was silent. Sam welcomed the silence. It was something he needed.

He took another breath, released it, then reached for his towel and wiped sweat from his face and neck. He laid the towel across his stomach and stared back up at the ceiling tile.

He said he'd do it.

He was still trying to come to grips with that. Still trying to deal with the fact that he had no choice.

Twelve years ago it could have all been different. He could have been sitting in the back of a police car, waiting to be taken to jail, instead of sitting at a table at Sal's Ristorante.

Sam closed his eyes and breathed slowly. The Top Forty music above him changed and became an Italian serenade. The scent of sweat disappeared and was replaced by food.

Sam opened his eyes. He was no longer at the gym, surrounded by equipment and emptiness. He was back in Sal's, sitting across from Zeke. They'd just come from the hospital. Sam's nose was bandaged, but not broken, and throbbing.

Unlike Sal's Pizzeria from Spike Lee's classic, *Do The Right Thing*, this Sal's had famous Blacks on the walls. They shook Sal's hand, draped their arms over his shoulders, and even gave him kisses on the cheeks and lips. Sal was genuinely well-liked and respected by his patrons.

Sam looked around at the décor. He'd never eaten in an establishment as fancy as Sal's. The closest he'd ever thought he'd get to being in a place like Sal's was by observing it through the glass as he stood outside on the city block, or seeing it on the television. Sal's and other places like it weren't for him. They were for the white, rich, and elite crowd. If black people were in there, it was only because they had "sold out" and lived life hating the color of their skin. That was the narrow view he'd grown up with.

He was a nigga, and he would never be anything but that.

Zeke was a nigga too. He just thought he was better than everyone with his fancy car, expensive clothes, and proper speech.

Sam gave Zeke a scowl as Zeke looked at him. He'd never liked being stared at. It made him uncomfortable. Made him feel as though he were being judged and ridiculed at the same time. He shifted in his seat, grabbed his menu and opened it.

"Pick anything you want," Zeke said, opening his.

Sam scoured the menu, looking at the prices listed beside each entrée. He looked up at Zeke.

"Twenty-five dollars for some damn ravioli?"

Zeke nodded.

Sam shook his head. "That don't even make sense."

Zeke laughed. "Just order."

Sam shrugged his shoulders. "Your dime," he said.

He looked back down at the menu. A few minutes later, the waitress, a heavy-set, clearly Italian female in her mid-twenties, came to take their orders. Sam settled on the rigatoni with meat sauce and a beer. Zeke, a frequent patron, was having his usual—fettuccine with shrimp, bathed in cream sauce with black olives and tomatoes. He ordered his favorite drink—Scotch—to go with it.

Silence hung in the air for a few seconds after the waitress walked away, until Sam asked, "Why didn't you call the cops?" It was a question he'd been wondering as he sat in Zeke's car on the way to the hospital, and then again on the way to the restaurant.

Zeke looked at him for a moment, and then reached for his cell phone. He said, "I can call now if you want me to?"

Sam watched him. He could tell by the look in Zeke's eyes that he was very serious. He shook his head. "Nah. It's cool."

"You sure," Zeke asked. "Because I can have them here in a few minutes."

Sam shook his head again. "It's cool. I was just wondering, that's all."

Zeke gave a nod and put his cell phone back down on the table. A second later, the waitress returned with their drinks. "Why didn't I call the police?" he said as the waitress walked away.

He wrapped his fingers around his glass. He loved Scotch. He loved its dry, bitter flavor. He loved the way it burned in the back of his throat and on its way down his chest. Were he an alcoholic, Scotch would be the drink he'd have to keep locked away in the cabinet, the whereabouts of the key unknown to him.

He raised the glass to his lips and took a sip, letting the liquid stir around in his mouth, before caressing its way down. He let out a satisfied, "Ah," and then focused back on Sam. "Don't you think there are enough black men in jail?" he asked.

Sam raised his eyebrows and scoffed. "More than enough."

"Believe it or not, jail used to have a purpose. It wasn't just about housing criminals. At one point, going to jail meant getting a second chance at life. An opportunity to not only do the time for the crime, but an opportunity to also reevaluate the path you were on. Guys went to jail and got informed. Informed about themselves and the system. Some guys got GEDs. Others, associate's and even bachelor's degrees. The ones who were fortunate enough to get out came out knowing that while life on the outside wasn't going to be easy, it wasn't over. It wasn't hopeless.

"Black men go to jail now, spend some time eating, working out, and watching cable, before they come out and go right back to doing what put them there in the first place. Let's face it, the word 'hardened' is no longer associated with the word 'criminal.' Jail is a cakewalk now. It's a badge of honor. You could even call it an aphrodisiac the way the ladies seem to flock to the guys who've done time. Why didn't I call the police?"

Zeke paused and grabbed his glass. He picked it up and swirled the liquid around, making the bits of ice clink.

Sam watched him. His nose was throbbing, but he hardly felt the pain. Zeke had him entranced. He'd been dead on with what he'd said: he wasn't scared of jail. That's why he'd been a repeat offender. Jail was a roof overhead for some. Temporary chill time for others. To some extent, Sam preferred jail to being out in the real world, because there was an order and discipline behind prison walls that didn't exist in the streets.

Sam stared at Zeke.

Zeke stared at Sam.

Why hadn't he called the police?

"You thought taking my money and my car was going to be easy." Zeke paused and took another sip of his Scotch.

Sam remained silent.

Zeke continued. "Obviously your nose and pride found out that it wasn't."

Zeke downed the rest of his drink.

"Calling the police on you and letting them take you to jail would have been too easy. It wouldn't have been a good enough punishment for disrespecting me."

"Punishment?" Sam looked at Zeke as though he were crazy. "Instead of calling the police, you bring me to this fancy restaurant. I'm sipping on a beer waiting for my grub. Shit . . . your idea of punishment is a hell of a lot different than mine."

Zeke flagged down the waitress for another drink and then looked at Sam and said, "I didn't just bring you here to feed you, Sam."

"No?"

"No."

"So then why are we here?"

"I want to offer you a job."

Sam pulled his head back a notch. "A job?"

"Yes."

"Yo . . . I just tried to rob you."

"I know. I was there, remember?"

"So then what you wanna offer me a job for?"

The waitress brought Zeke his other drink, as well as their food. Zeke waited until she walked away to reply.

"Jail was getting off easy for you, Sam. You wanted the fast money. You wanted the fast car. I'm going to show you how you can have those things, by working for them. Work is the real punishment for you young guys today. That's why the jails are overflowing. You guys want things the easy way. You don't want to work for anything. And because you don't, you have no real concept of what value is. Without the understanding of value, you all have no pride. Without pride, you all continue to disrespect yourselves and others, and as you do that, more and more of you get thrown in jails so overcrowded, there's no real opportunity to be rehabilitated into being contributing members of society. The funds, time, and, quite frankly, the desire by the system and people employed by it to help turn your lives around just isn't there."

Zeke stopped talking and grabbed his fork to start eating. Sam's stomach rumbled. He couldn't remember the last time he'd had a real meal. He grabbed his fork and began to eat his spaghetti.

Zeke swallowed a forkful of his fettuccine, washed it down with Scotch, and then held up his fork.

"This is your toughest challenge, Sam. You want the things I have, then this is your shot. Living without pride, living without a true understanding of value is easy. It's like waking up and rolling from your back to your side and doing nothing all day. I'm giving you an opportunity to open your eyes, get out of bed, and strive for something better."

Sam looked at the fork and then back at Zeke, who was taking another mouthful of food. The fork in the road, he thought. A chance at having more in life. He said, "What happens if I turn the offer down?"

"Then I call the police right now."

Sam looked at Zeke.

Zeke stared back, his eyes as unflinching and deadpan as his tone had been.

"So, basically I have no choice?"

Zeke shook his head. "Oh, you have a choice, Sam. A clear choice."

Zeke picked up a forkful of spaghetti and slid it into his mouth. One week later, after clearing it with his parole officer, Sam was working in the mailroom, earning a marginal but real paycheck. He may not have known it about himself, but Zeke had seen something special in him. Just as Zeke expected, Sam worked his way up the corporate ladder over a six-year span to become head of marketing, answering only to Zeke, who he looked to not only as a friend, but as a father figure.

One year later, after Jewell finally ended what he'd quietly observed as a relationship destined to fail, Sam received Zeke's blessing to ask his daughter, who'd been as attracted to Sam as he'd been to her, on a date. Six months after their first date, Zeke became Sam's father-in-law.

Now he was making well over six figures, living in a six-bedroom home with a ten-foot deep pool in the back. This was the life Zeke had promised he could have if he worked for it.

Sam sighed and sat up from the bench. *All this time*, he thought. *All this time I've been living on borrowed time.*

Because of his criminal record, Sam hadn't been able to acquire anything on his own, so over the years, Zeke assisted him by either buying or co-signing for the things he owned.

Or thought he owned.

The cars. The home. His credit cards. His job.

Until the ultimatum, he'd been living his life as though it had been his own, when it had never been his life at all.

Sam wiped sweat away from his forehead. Stress, not the workout, was making him perspire now. He should have never given in to the advances. But she'd promised to go down on him. Said she would swallow him. Let him have her in any position he wanted. She'd wanted it hard, rough. She'd wanted it to hurt. Her promises to do and take it all had driven him wild. He wanted Jewell to let go that way, but she never did. He had been OK with it for a while, but the routine sex had eventually gotten to him, and he found himself becoming weaker as each day passed. His eyes began to wander more and more. He'd resisted until the intern arrived. Now his mother-in-law—a woman he respected and liked, even loved—had to die. To avoid his own death—because surely to go back to having nothing was comparable—there was no other option. As much as he wished there were, the fact was there were no other choices available.

Sapphire had to die so that he could continue to live.

His cell phone chimed suddenly, causing him to jump. He reached into the pocket of his sweat pants, pulled it out and looked at the caller ID. He expected it to be Jewell wondering why he had been taking so long.

It wasn't her.

He took a breath, hit the talk button, exhaled, and said, "Yeah?"

On the other end, Zeke said, "I want you to shoot her. In the heart."

Chapter 11

"**I** want him killed, too."

Zeke stopped talking and pressed up and down on the top of the Bic pen he held in his hand. He sat behind his office desk in near darkness, save for a small lamp to his right illuminating the room in an ominous yellow, and the moonlight shining through the window. Spread out in front of him were the photographs of Sapphire and the other man. His head had been cut off in the photographs, signifying that his role was small in the grand scheme of things. His wife was having an affair and that's what mattered. With whom was inconsequential.

But Sapphire's lie to him changed everything.

Prior to then, he'd had only the photographs. Without question the photos had been all the proof he needed. But before her lie, Sapphire still had an out. She still had the ability to deny what his eyes had seen over and over and over again. Before the lie, if confronted with the glossy 8x11s, Sapphire could have said that someone had been trying to set her up. That the photographs had been Photo-shopped.

She would never disrespect the vows she'd sworn be-fore God and before family. She loved Zeke too much to betray him that way. How could he ever think that after everything they'd been through, that after the life they'd built together . . . how could he possibly believe she would do something like that?

Photoshopped.

Her head placed on someone else's body.

Couldn't he tell?

But what about the lips?

You've kissed these lips a thousand times. Can't you see the difference?

I . . . I . . . yes. I suppose I can see it. The bottom lip is a little smaller. But the eyes . . . They look just like yours.

Mine aren't as slanted. Can't you tell?

I . . . I don't know.

What do you mean you don't know? You don't recog-nize my body, my lips, my eyes . . . Do you pay any at-tention to me at all?

I . . . of course I do. The pictures just seemed so real.

Well, they're not, Zeke! They're not real!

I . . . I see that now. I can see the difference.

Can you?

Yes.

Are you sure?

Yes.

I would never betray you, Ezekiel. Never!

I know. And I'm sorry for questioning you.

Burn those photographs, Zeke. Burn them. I don't ever want them to be brought up again.

OK.

I love you, Zeke. Do you believe that?

Yes. Yes, I do. And I love you too.

You have nothing to worry about, Ezekiel. My love is real. No other man could ever come between us, OK?

OK.

You're my husband. I'm your wife, and our bond is secure. Don't ever think it's not.

I won't.

You promise?

I do.

Burn those photographs, Zeke. Burn them and get those images out of your mind, because they're not real.

I . . . I will.

Before the lie, that's how the conversation should have gone. Before the lie, she had an out. It was slim, but it was there. But she said that she had been at Marlene's house right after he'd seen her come out of the apartment building and walk across the street.

She'd lied.

It was over the phone, but he'd felt as though she'd been standing in front of him, looking at him face to face.

She'd lied, and that made the anger, resentment, pain, and bitterness inside of him burn even more. He'd wanted her dead, yes. But now he wanted her to suffer. He'd wanted her to feel the pain she'd caused him. This was the decision he'd made after she'd gone back into the building.

"I want her to know why she's dying. I want her to know that I wanted her to die. I want her heart to break just before her life is taken."

Still on the bench at the gym, Sam shook his head.

"Zeke . . . this is . . ." He paused. Chills came over him as a result of the intensely serious insanity in Zeke's voice. "It doesn't have to be this way, Zeke," he finally said.

"There is no other way, Sam," Zeke said. "She betrayed me. You betrayed my daughter. This is the price you both have to pay for that betrayal."

"But, Zeke . . ." Sam paused again. He'd agreed to do it, but in the back of his mind there'd been a glimmer of hope that Zeke would come to his senses and realize that he could no longer continue to let his emotions rule his rationale. He was angry and hurt, but surely his bark was worse than his bite. "Zeke . . . you're talking about murder."

"Are you backing out, Sam?"

Sam clenched his jaws and squeezed his cell phone so hard it groaned in his hand and threatened to break.

Was he backing out?

He clenched his jaws again. He wanted to so badly.

"This is payback, Sam. An eye for an eye. This is justice for all that I've done. I put my all into building the life Sapphire has come to enjoy. Everything she has. Everything she does. It's all because of the time I've sacrificed. I never asked anything of her. All I wanted was her love and support. That's all I ever needed from her, because that's all it took to keep me whole. That's all it took to keep me sane. Loyalty, Sam. That's all I needed. But she betrayed me, and so did you."

"Zeke—"

"I gave you my daughter's hand, Sam, under the pretense that she would always be the most important thing in your life."

Sam breathed out. "She is, Zeke. I swear."

"Bullshit, Sam! That's bullshit!"

"Zeke—"

"You want to talk about murder, Sam? Well, guess what . . . if anyone should be associated with that, it should be my wife. Because I'm dead, Sam. I died the day those pictures came, and there's no one to blame for my death but Sapphire. My heart, my soul, my spirit—she shattered them. She's the goddamned murderer! She's the villain in the false love affair that I've been living. She has to pay and so do you."

"But, Zeke—"

Zeke slammed his fist down on his desktop. "I gave you everything, you son of a bitch! You wouldn't have shit had I never given you that job!"

"I know, Zeke," Sam said, cradling his forehead in his hand.

"I could have had you locked away, but I gave you a chance. I gave you an opportunity to become something other than the nigga you were."

Zeke let out a growl and violently swept the photos from the desk.

"You owe everything to me, you piece of shit!" Zeke raged.

Sam sighed and said, "I know, Zeke."

"Your house. Your cars. Your credit cards. The job you have. You would have nothing if I didn't purchase it or put my name behind it."

"I know," Sam said again.

"I trusted you, Sam. I put my name behind you. I walked my daughter down the aisle to you. Sapphire fucked another man. You fucked another woman. Somewhere down the line, you would have done to my daughter what that goddamned bitch did to me! Somewhere down the line, my little princess would have been devastated and broken inside. You have to pay, Sam. For what you did and for what you would have done . . . you have to pay. You will kill Sapphire. You will make her suffer before you do, or your life as you know it will be over."

Zeke paused and stared daggers at the photographs on the floor, his eyes fixed on Sapphire. Fixed on the expression on her face. He forced himself to take a slow, deep breath. He wanted Sam to be there in the office with him. Anger had him boiling inside. He wanted to hurt Sam. Wanted to punch him, kick him, choke him. He wanted to lose the control he'd been struggling to maintain. He wanted to let loose the anger.

He stared at the picture. Stared at Sapphire as she bit down on her lip.

He breathed.

He couldn't lose control.

His sanity was riding on not losing what little of himself he had left.

He took another breath and said, "Next Saturday. That's when I want it done."

Sam dropped his hand from his face. "Next Saturday?"

"Yes."

"But that's . . . that's not enough time.

"That's all the time you're going to get, Sam."

Sam shook his head. "Christ, Zeke."

Sam clenched his jaws. He'd hurt others before, in his other life—back when he didn't respect it and didn't respect others. He'd knocked people unconscious. He'd fractured and broken bones. Before Zeke, Sam had the potential to graduate from being a typical street thug who could talk the killer's talk, but never had the guts to walk the walk, to becoming a thug without fear, without remorse.

That was the path he'd been on.

Walking in a tunnel with no light in sight. Just darkness. Miles and miles of it. But then Zeke stepped out of the shadows with a candle in his hand and a promise to lead him out to safety. All he had to do was follow, and that's just what he did.

The path wasn't always easy. On more than one occasion, the lure of the streets and the fast money to be made called out to him, promising that if he took a step back into the shadows one more time he would come out like a champ, because he was going to do it big. But despite the pull back to negativity, Sam resisted and continued to follow the candlelight.

Before Zeke, Sam could have committed murder.

But things were different now. He was different.

He clenched his jaws. "Zeke . . . come on . . ."

"Tell me no, Sam. Say it and I'll come and pick you up and drop you off at your old neighborhood. Say no. Tell me that you won't do it."

Sam's throat went dry. His head began to hurt at the temples. Stress and anxiety hammering.

Say no.

He looked around and was glad to see that he was alone by the free weights. "I . . . I can't . . ." he said before his voice trailed off.

Zeke reached down and grabbed a photograph from the floor. Sapphire was looking into the camera, staring at him, mocking him. His fist closed around the photo at the sides, causing it to wrinkle.

Sam barely breathed, the throbbing in his temples becoming sharper. He began to feel pain behind his right eye: signs of a migraine coming. Tension ran down from his neck, through his shoulders, down his back.

"Can't what, Sam?" Zeke asked. His heart ached for what he was putting his son-in-law through. He respected, Sam. Respected the fight in him. Respected the desire Sam had to want and become more. He admired his will and determination. He hated to do this to him, but he had no choice. Betrayal burned Zeke at his core. He was screaming on the inside a thousand times over.

Betrayal.

As far as Zeke was concerned, betrayal's sting was worse than the pain of losing a loved one, because he would forever feel its effects. With death there was pain, but over time, that pain would subside. He would miss the loved one, but the certainty of the fact that the person would no longer be coming back was reassuring. He would never have to wonder why, if, when, or how. Death was final. You experienced it, you accepted it, and you moved on.

The same couldn't be said for betrayal. Sure, he could say that he would accept it for what it was. That despite how badly he was hurting, he would agree to forgive and leave the past behind. But as was the case with death, with betrayal there was no reassurance that he wouldn't relive the pain. The why, if, when, and how would remain in the back of his mind, causing a thick, dark cloud of doubt to hover overhead. Every day, whether he remained with the purveyor of the crime, those questions would tear away pieces of his soul little by little, which would ultimately transform him from being the person he once was, to being a harder, colder, or possibly weaker, more broken individual.

Zeke didn't want that for himself.

He didn't want that for Jewell.

At some point, she would go through what he was going through because even before it happened to him, he'd always felt that things done in the dark eventually came to light. From the day his little girl entered this world, he swore to always protect her. Holding her six pound body in his arms for the first time, he promised her with a kiss on her tiny forehead that no one would ever hurt her, and if anyone ever did, he'd make them pay.

Betrayal.

He loved Sam as though he'd been conceived from his own sperm, but he'd fucked the intern. Things done in the dark . . . At some point, his little princess was going to have to deal with his infidelity. He couldn't and wouldn't allow that.

"Can't what, Sam?"

Sam struggled to draw a breath. He wanted to say it so badly. He opened his mouth to say it. But he couldn't. "I . . . can't say no."

All of the air sighed from his lungs as his shoulders sagged. As much as he wanted to . . . he just couldn't. He loved his life too much. The cars, the home, the money, the status. He was somebody with a bunch of somethings. He'd lived so hard at the opposite end of the equation. He'd been down and dirty. He'd been spat on for so long. The intern meant nothing to him.

He took a breath and released it slowly. It was selfish, but he couldn't and wouldn't give up his life over a meaningless thrill.

"I can't say no," he said again, his voice just above a whisper.

Zeke bent down and picked up another photograph. Sapphire was holding her breast and arching her back as she rode the other man. The scene played out in his head. He could see her moving. He could hear her moaning,

begging for more. His hands began to shake as the porno-
graphic moment flashed over and over in blood red behind his eyes.

He said, "Next Friday is going to be my anniversary,
Sam. It will represent a new beginning that I am going to
cherish. Sapphire's death on that day will mark the beginning of a new life for me. A new life that I have to have. I
want it done on that day. No exceptions."

"Won't you be with her?"

"No."

Sam nodded. "The man in the picture . . . do you know
who he is?"

"No."

"Don't you want to know?"

"No."

Sam nodded and then looked to his right as another
gentleman walked into the free-weight area. He and the
man exchanged nods.

Lowering his voice, he said, "Next Friday?"

"Next Friday."

Sam gritted his teeth. "OK."

Chapter 12

One hour later, Sam was staring into Jewell's eyes as he moved inside of her vigorously. Jewell was sitting on top of him, taking all that he had to give. Taking it deep, taking it hard. Damn hard.

So hard it began to hurt.

She looked at him and said, "Easy, baby. Easy."

But Sam didn't hear her.

He was there in their master bedroom with desert sun–colored walls, bordered by white olive trim. Colors Jewell just had to have because they reminded her of the sun and sand from their vacation in Trinidad earlier in the year. He was there in the room, on the bed, naked and inside of his wife, his hands clamped around her hips, lifting her up on his hard shaft, and then pulling her back down as he thrust upward.

He was there as Jewell said again, "Easy, Sam. Not so hard."

He was there. Physically. But mentally . . .

Mentally, he was far away.

He was somewhere locked away in a dimly lit room, padded with white foam. His arms were crisscrossed and pinned to his chest by a straightjacket from which couldn't break free.

In this room, Sam screamed, cursed, and growled. His head ached from the tumultuous clamor, as though someone were beating on church bells right beside his ear. Sharp pain stabbed at his temples, intensifying the noise, and frustration plagued his spirit.

On top of him, Jewell called out his name again. "Sam . . . take it easy. You're hurting me. Stop!"

Sam's grip around his wife's hips tightened. He lifted her up, brought her back down. With each thrust he thought about what he had to do.

One week.

The straps on the straightjacket tightened. He tried to take a breath, but it was hard and labored. The walls around him began to close suddenly, making breathing that much harder. Sam screamed, cursed, and growled louder in his mind. He fucked his wife harder, causing her to cry out again.

"Sam, stop!"

Jewell tried to push herself off of him, but to no avail. Sam's fingers were viced and locked.

Jewell called out his name again. "Sam!"

She squirmed and pounded on his chest two times before the white padded walls disappeared.

For the first time since sliding inside of his wife, Sam remembered where he was. He unclasped his fingers from around her hips and said, "Shit."

Jewell slapped him hard across his face. "Asshole!" She

slapped him again and then climbed off of him. "You ass-hole! What the hell was wrong with you?"

She got out of the bed, stood on wobbly legs and hur-ried into the bathroom, slamming the door and locking it behind her.

Sam said, "Shit," again, then climbed out of the bed and went to the bathroom door. "Jewell . . . shit . . . Jewell, open the door."

"Leave me alone, Sam," Jewell said, her voice trem-bling. Tears were falling from her eyes. She slammed down the toilet seat and sat down. She couldn't believe what had just happened. Had she just been raped by her husband? She wrapped her arms around herself. Her vagina throbbed from the pounding. She dropped her chin to her chest and leaned forward, and wondered again what the hell had just happened.

Sam knocked on the door. "Come on, Jewell."

"I told you to leave me alone, Sam."

Sam let out a sigh. "Jewell, I'm . . . I'm sorry."

Jewell lifted her head and looked toward the door. "You're sorry? You practically raped me, you son of a bitch!"

"Come on," Sam said. "You're exaggerating a little bit."

"Exaggerating? I told you to stop!"

Sam leaned his forehead against the door. He was just as shocked as she. One minute he'd been inside of her, using the sex to release pent-up frustration, and the next minute he was on the verge of suffocating and losing his mind. He sighed again. She had every right to be angry.

It may not have been rape in the truest sense, but it had been close enough. He'd lost it. He clenched his jaws and damned himself for the predicament he'd brought on.

Jewell was the perfect woman. She had been from the first moment he'd laid eyes on her, back when he'd been no one. Just a guy working in the mailroom. That was when he'd first noticed her. She'd come in to see her father—something she did on a tri-weekly basis back then. She and Zeke had always been close.

Sapphire may have carried and delivered Jewell, but she never came close to connecting with her in the way Zeke had. They were father and daughter, but in an odd way, they were soul mates of sorts. Kindred spirits: that was the phrase Zeke often used when describing his relationship with his little princess. From the day Jewell was born, they were engulfed in a love affair that was immeasurably true and pure.

Kindred spirits, able to talk about anything. When Jewell had problems in school, it was her father she ran to. When she became a woman in the truest form, it was Zeke she confided in first. And when the boys came knocking and she reached the point where she wanted to open the door, it was from Zeke she sought advice and permission.

Her connection with her father hadn't been forced. It had just always been there. Their close relationship had always been the source of the great divide with Jewell and her mother. As Jewell grew older, the divide grew wider.

Sapphire would never admit it, but she was jealous of her daughter. Even as a little girl, Jewell had been beautiful, charming, and graceful. Those qualities about her were only enhanced as she grew older. Although her interaction with her father had never been inappropriate in any way, Sapphire viewed her daughter as the other woman. Sapphire had Zeke's love and devotion, but she never had his heart the way Jewell did, and that knowledge kept Sapphire from ever being able to be close to her daughter without feeling pangs of jealousy lingering just beneath the surface. Because of this, Jewell grew up at arm's length from her mother, while she burrowed closer and closer to her father.

The day Sam first laid eyes on her, Jewell had come in to the office to make sure that her father had been taking it easy. He'd recently been told by his doctor that his blood pressure was high, so Jewell had come in to make sure he wasn't overdoing it. Sam had been delivering mail at that time, and when he saw her, everything and everyone around him seemed to freeze. He'd seen fine women before, but never had he come across a beauty as natural and almost angelic. Her eyes—intense and soft. Her smile— captivatingly sexy. Her curves—soft-lined and toned. He'd heard people talk about love at first sight, but until that very moment, he never truly understood just what it was.

He wanted to approach her on that first day, but he knew he had to bring something to the table. Jewell was the spitting image of her mother, but her personality had been carbon copied from Zeke, so Sam knew there could be no half-stepping to win her heart. He had to be a man— all man. So while he admired her from afar, he busted his ass gaining Zeke's trust, friendship, and respect as he worked his way up the corporate ladder.

Unfortunately for Sam, when he thought he had been ready finally to step up to the plate and make his move, Jewell showed up at the office with a new man on her arm.

Unable to pursue her romantically, Sam opted to become a good friend, while hoping for the opportunity to be there for her when the relationship—which he'd always seemed to know wouldn't last—ended. When the day finally came, he didn't hesitate to make his move.

What he didn't know at the time was that the move he would have to make would be a very small one, because just as he had been taken by her, Jewell had been feeling him from day one.

She'd dated infrequently during the time Sam spent grooming himself to become the man she would eventually marry. Just as much as Sam had felt the instant connection when he'd first seen her, Jewell had felt it too. When she dated her eventual ex, she'd been into the relationship full throttle, because, just like her father, she never did anything half-assed. However, just as Sam had known, she too had the notion that it wouldn't last.

A person's eyes are the windows to her soul.

Her father had always told her that. He'd always said that if you looked close enough and truly paid attention, you would know all you needed to know about someone. You could see his faults, his good and bad intentions. Her ex had wolf's eyes, but she'd allowed his good looks, charm, and status in the business world to blind her.

But when it came to Sam . . .

He hadn't been the only one frozen in suspended animation that first day. Jewell had stared long and hard at Sam, and into his eyes. Eyes that revealed a gentle and loving soul despite a rough past. Eyes that were deep and intense.

Neither of them could fully explain how and why, but they both knew on that day that they were meant to be together.

Now, Sam clenched his jaws again and knocked lightly on the bathroom door. He'd fucked up, and not just with the sex gone wrong. "Jewell," he said softly, "please open the door." He knew she wasn't going to, but he still had to try.

"Leave me alone, Sam," Jewell replied. She wiped tears from her eyes and reached over to run a bath.

"Jewell . . . please. I'm sorry. Please come back to bed."

Jewell opened her mouth to respond and then closed it, then stood up and looked at herself in the mirror over the sink. She was shaking. No one knew, but years ago, her ex had forced himself on her. It was at the end of the relationship. His ego was bruised because she'd said things were over between them. He cursed and ranted about how no female had ever ended things with him because he was the ultimate catch. He was pissed, and with his anger, embarrassment, and frustration brewing, he forced himself on her. Jewell fought with everything she had to get him off, but it had been to no avail, and in the end she eventually lay still and let him show her what she was "giving up." She'd never told anyone about what had occurred, and eventually she'd learn to bury the incident deep down.

She shook again as chills came over her. On some level, she'd exaggerated what had just happened. Sam was her husband and he loved her. What had occurred wasn't out of anger. But if not anger . . . what then? She looked at herself in the mirror for a second longer and then, after a sigh, moved to the tub to check the water level.

On the opposite side of the door, Sam stood with his forehead pressed against the wood and listened to the running water. He wanted to call Jewell's name again, but he knew there was no point to it. He exhaled, backed away from the door, and went to the bed. He clenched his jaws one more time, closed his fists tightly, and again envisioned himself in the straightjacket, locked away in the room padded with white foam. Things were unraveling.

One week.

To keep his peace.

To keep his sanity.

One week.

He took a deep breath, released it slowly, then opened his fists. He took one last look over his shoulder to the bathroom door. Jewell was in the tub now. Sam cursed himself and the intern, and then grabbed a pillow and walked out of the bedroom.

That night he would sleep on the couch.

The next day he would begin to do what he had to do to keep from going crazy.

Saturday—Six Days

Chapter 13

"Hello, Jewell."

"Mom. What are you doing here?"

Jewell stared at her mother with hard eyes and her lips tight.

Sapphire felt the glare as though beams of heat were coming from them and boring holes into her flesh. She stepped past her daughter.

Jewell clenched her jaws, forced herself to take a calming breath, closed the front door, and turned around to face her mother.

"Did I interrupt your workout?"

Jewell wiped beads of sweat from her forehead. She'd been forty-five minutes into her ninety-minute workout. She was doing step aerobics with kickboxing, a workout routine she'd learned in her kickboxing class at the gym. The instructor of her class, Lisette, was fierce, no-nonsense, and took no prisoners. Jewell had been taking the class for a full month and had already lost five of the ten pounds she wanted to lose, and had toned up considerably.

She hadn't really been out of shape before she joined the weekly Monday seven-thirty PM classes, but she had some tightening up to do. Lisette demanded a lot from her class. Working out, Jewell had been trying to match Lisette's intensity kick-punch for kick-punch. She hadn't wanted to stop when she heard the doorbell chime, but her focus was gone after the third chime, so she gave in. Staring at her mother now, she wished she would have just continued.

She wiped more perspiration away and said, "I was just about done."

Her mother nodded.

"So . . . what are you doing here?" Jewell asked.

Her mother removed her coat and walked to the living room. "Where's Sam?"

"He's not here."

"Working?"

Jewell shrugged her shoulders. "Not sure."

She'd been hoping to talk to him and explain why she'd reacted the way she had to the sex the night before, but he'd slept on the couch, and when she'd woken up, he'd already left the house. "I think he had some errands to run. Is that why you're here? To see Sam?"

Sapphire shook her head. She noticed sadness in her daughter's eyes. She wanted to probe, to ask if things were all right between them, but she didn't have that type of relationship with her daughter. Sapphire's hope was that this visit would change that, or at the very least, be the catalyst to establishing a tighter bond between them.

A few nights before, she'd found old Polaroid photographs of a family trip to Niagara Falls. Jewell had been three years old then, and in one of the photographs she beamed with an innocent and loving smile. Zeke had been standing behind Sapphire making funny faces at Jewell, prompting the bright smile.

Alone in her house, Sapphire shed tears while she looked at the series of pictures of Jewell posing alone, or posing with her father. There were none of her and her daughter, and that's what brought the tears. Looking at the pictures, Sapphire couldn't help but wonder had she taken any pictures with her daughter instead of remaining behind the camera with pangs of jealousy festering inside, if things would have been different between them from that point on.

Sapphire said, "I came to see you."

Jewell eyed her mother skeptically. "Me? Why?"

"You usually come by the house at least once, sometimes twice a week, but you haven't been by lately."

Jewell looked at her mother as images of her with her gigolo flashed in her mind. "I've been . . . busy," she said, a sharp edge to her tone.

"Busy doing?"

Jewell let out a breath laced with irritation. "Just busy, Mom."

Sapphire frowned. "Jewell . . . I know we don't have the closest of relationships, but you can talk to me, you know. Your father's not the only one who's interested in things going on in your life. If things between you and Sam are a little strained, maybe I can offer some advice."

Jewell passed her tongue along the front of her top teeth. She was doing all she could to keep from going off on her mother, but the longer her mother stood in front of her, the harder it was to keep her tongue in check.

You pay for sex, you ungrateful, disgusting bitch, she wanted to scream.

Instead, she said, "Mom . . . there's nothing to tell. Sam and I are fine. I've just been busy."

"All I'm asking is busy doing what, Jewell?"

Jewell passed her tongue across her teeth again. "Let's do this another day, Mom, OK? I've got some things to do, places to go, and I'm quite sure you do too."

Sapphire eyed her daughter curiously. "What do you mean by that?"

"By what?"

"I have places to get to."

Jewell clenched her jaws. She shook her head, and said, "Nothing," and then bit down on her tongue.

"It sounded like you were insinuating *something*," Sapphire said, looking at Jewell intensely.

"What could I possibly have to insinuate, Mom? Are you guilty of something?"

Sapphire watched her daughter. Something in Jewell's eyes, something about the way she stared back . . . Her stare seemed to be much more than just a stare.

"Guilty? What would I have to be guilty of?"

"I don't know . . . you're the one talking about me insinuating something."

Tense silence passed between mother and daughter, as both eyed one another. Anger brewed just beneath Jewell's surface, making her perspire more, despite her inactivity. Sapphire was warm with angst and nervousness. Perhaps her daughter's words were just that—words. Still . . . Sapphire couldn't shake the feeling there'd been more to them.

"I'm not guilty of anything," she said.

Jewell raised her eyebrows. "Well, then I wasn't insinuating that you were."

Mother and daughter looked at one another in silence again, their eyes saying more than any words could or would say.

Sapphire thought about the old pictures of her little girl and wished she could have gone back to that day in front of the Falls. She'd take multiple photos with Jewell in her arms this time, and she'd shower her with kisses. Things would be different from then on. Sapphire stared, wished, and sighed. The past was the past. The present was what it was, and despite what she'd hoped, the future didn't look promising. Not for them. At least not now. Not this time.

Sapphire sighed. "I just want us to be closer, Jewell. That's why I'm here."

Jewell shook her head. "Not today, Mom."

"Is it even possible for us?" Sapphire asked sincerely.

"Not today, Mom," Jewell said again. "Let's not do this today."

"I was looking at some old pictures the other day."

"Mom—"

"We were at Niagara Falls. Do you remember that day?"

Jewell sighed. She didn't want to take any trips down memory lane. "Mom . . . I have—"

"You probably don't remember that trip. You were only three then."

"Mom, please . . ." Jewell tried again.

"Jewell, we're not the closest, and I know . . . I know that's more my fault than yours."

Jewell wiped sweat away from her forehead again. Before the discovery of her mother's affair, before the photos, she would have been willing to sit and talk, perhaps over hot tea or hot chocolate, to try to make the distance between them go away. The majority of her friends had close relationships with their mothers, and that was something Jewell envied. The bond she shared with her father was truly a special one, but because he was a male, there were certain things he just couldn't relate to emotionally. He couldn't completely understand her desires, her needs. He would get it, but not "get it." Not in the way her mother would or should have. Before the discovery, Jewell would have listened, talked, even forgiven.

But now . . .

"Mom . . . some other time . . . maybe we could have talked. But right now I'm not in the mood. Besides, I have things to do."

Sapphire was taken aback. Without having been touched physically, Jewell's callous tone and attitude had hit her like a sharp slap in the face. "Are these things more important than us talking?" She sighed and thought about the Niagara Falls photographs again, wishing one more time for Hiro's power from the television show *Heroes*. But that was fantasy and no matter how hard she tried to focus, she wasn't going to acquire the ability to turn back the clock anytime soon. Reality was what it was, and it was pointless to push the issue anymore. She looked at her daughter, frowned, and said, "OK."

Jewell nodded, and without a word, walked past her mother, went to the front door, and opened it. Sapphire slipped her coat back on and went to the door. Just before crossing the threshold, she paused and looked at her daughter again. She wanted to say something, but the tight-lipped expression on Jewell's face kept her silent. With a defeated exhale, she stepped outside, and as the door closed shut behind her, she wondered if she and her daughter would ever become friends.

On the other side of the door, Jewell breathed in and out deeply. She needed to kick and punch again. She needed to let out the anger and disgust she was holding inside. She turned and headed back to start over the workout DVD from the beginning.

Sunday—Five Days

Chapter 14

Sam was back in his old neighborhood. Not because he wanted to be, but because he had to be. He had one week to make things happen. One week to hurt Jewell, but to be there for her through the hurt. It wasn't going to be easy, but at least he was going to be around. His life was still going to be his. That's what mattered.

His mother-in-law didn't.

That was the way he'd come to look at things. It had been the only way to look at things. It wasn't about Zeke. Or Sapphire. Or Jewell.

It was about his life.

It was about a past to which he couldn't and wouldn't go back.

Sam turned right onto a block littered with row homes, double-parked in front of one toward the end of the block, and kept the engine running. A few seconds later, someone tapped on his passenger window. Sam unlocked the doors, then after his passenger got inside, put the car in drive and took off slowly. He made a right onto the next block, looked in his rear view, and, when he was certain that no one had followed them, held out a closed fist for a pound.

" 'Sup, Ty."

Ty Streets put his fist on top of Sam's. "Been a long time, nigga."

Sam kept his eyes on the road. "A long time," he agreed.

"I see you doin' a'ight for yourself."

Sam nodded. "I'm good."

"Shit . . . we all good, nigga. Make a right on the next block, then a left at the first alleyway. Go to the end of the alley, make a right, and then pull into the garage on the left."

"Old Man Hop still running that chop shop?"

"Ah, so you ain't forget where you came from."

As much as Sam wanted to . . ."Nah. I didn't forget."

"You just forgot about us ma'fuckas, then."

Sam didn't respond and kept focused on the street.

Ty was two years older than Sam and at least six inches taller, and fifty pounds heavier. Back in the day, he was known as The Black Hulk, not only because of his size, but also because of his rage. Ty had always been a step away from crazy, and those who knew better knew to keep him as far away from that step as possible.

Sam got to know Ty when they were both lookouts on the block. One night, four guys from a rivaling block jumped Ty as he was heading to the corner store. Ty had slept with the girlfriend of one of the guys and he wanted payback. Although it hadn't been easy, the four guys managed to beat Ty down until he was lying on the ground barely conscious. Standing over Ty with a .22 pointed at his head, the disgraced thug laughed and mocked about how he'd taken down The Black Hulk. Seconds before he pulled the trigger, Sam, who'd been on his way to see a girl he used to mess with from time to time, saw what was about to happen, and pulled out his weapon, shooting the thug in the head and killing him instantly. The other three guys, who'd been full of bravado only moments before, practically tripped over one another as they ran away.

Ty would have died that night, had it not been for Sam. From that moment on, they were as tight as could be. But when Ty was sentenced to prison for ten years for his second armed robbery offense, the two had lost touch.

"That ain't the old man's spot no more. He died two years ago."

"Old Man Hop was a good guy. Who's running it now?"

Ty laughed. "Couple of crooked-ass cops."

Sam turned and looked at Ty. "Word?"

Ty nodded. "Yeah. One of 'em is Hop's nephew. After Hop died, he and his partner took over the shop. They didn't take a cut before out of respect for Hop, but they kept the heat away. Now that Hop's ass is dead—"

"They still protect and get served in the progress."

"Yeah. Them niggas be rippin' us off, too."

"Damn."

"Anyway. It's a good spot to talk business."

"Why can't we talk here?"

"I got two niggas there waiting. My generals. Whatever you got to say to me, you can say in front of them niggas too."

" 'Sup, man, you don't trust me?"

Ty looked him over. "Been a long time, nigga."

"I'm still me though, Ty."

Ty looked him up and down, perusing his clothing, his

Movado watch, and platinum wedding band. "Nah, nigga
. . . you ain't the same."

Minutes later, Sam pulled into the chop shop and cut
the engine. Standing outside of the car were two guys—
one black, the other a Latino, with glocks in their hands.
Ty got out of the car first. Sam thought about calling the
whole thing off for a fleeting moment, but then got out of
the car. He'd made the call. He was there. There was no
turning back.

Ty pointed to his black partner, a thin guy with a jagged
scar running down the right side of his face. "Pat him
down, G."

Sam looked over at Ty. "Come on, man."

Ty shook his head. "Like I said, nigga. You ain't the
same."

Sam frowned and then spread his arms as G stepped to
him and groped him everywhere, checking for a weapon
or wire.

"He's cool," G said, stepping away from him seconds
later.

Ty gave him a nod and then looked over at the Latino.
"Loc' . . . check the car."

Sam opened his mouth to protest, but Ty cut him off.

"I'm sure you got insurance, nigga. Just tell 'em your
shit got broken into. You'll be a'ight."

Sam clenched his jaws and sighed. There was no point
in replying. Whether he liked it or not, his car was due for
an inspection. Fifteen minutes later, after his leather seats
had been ripped up, his glove compartment rifled through,
and his trunk searched, Loc' gave a thumbs-up signal and
said, "Cool."

"I told you you had nothing to worry about," Sam said,
glancing at the vandalism of his car's interior.

Ty shook his head again. "You clean, but you ain't the same nigga I came up with. You ain't got that same look in your eyes. You ain't hungry no more."

Sam looked from Ty to G to Loc' and then back to Ty. They were all staring at him, their eyes reflecting pain, abandonment, anger, distrust, and hopelessness. Feelings Sam had once known all too well. In another life, Sam's eyes bore the same reflection. He'd felt the same frustrations. People talked about heaven and hell, but in the lives Ty and his crew were living, hell was all they knew. Heaven was just a word that meant nothing. Until Zeke stepped into Sam's world, heaven had been just that for him, too.

Ty said Sam had changed, and standing there in front of Ty, Sam realized for the first time how true that statement was. He thought he'd been keeping things real all this time, but looking back at Ty, he saw just how much his reality had been skewed.

He gave Ty a conciliatory nod.

Ty nodded back, and said, "So what's up?"

Sam's heart beat heavily. This moment was the moment. *No turning back*, he thought again.

His heart thudded as he looked at Ty. After the night he'd saved Ty's life, Ty had been indebted to him, but never had Sam cashed in on that debt. Now, as he stood silent and still, his palms damp and cold, as much as he didn't want to do it, he knew the time had come.

"You remember when I shot that dude in the head?"

Ty closed his eyes a fraction. "Yeah."

"It's time for you to return the favor."

Monday—Four Days

Chapter 15

"Let's go out to dinner."

Sapphire looked up from a book she was reading. Zeke had just stepped into the bedroom. He'd been standing in the doorway watching her for several seconds. "Dinner? When?"

"An hour from now. I made reservations."

"Reservations? What's the occasion?"

"Nothing special. I just want to have dinner and drinks with my wife."

Sapphire looked at him. "Dinner? This is really last minute."

"It was a last-minute decision."

"I really don't have anything to wear."

"You have a ton of things to wear."

"But, Zeke—"

"Sapph . . . do you really have to put up a fight about me wanting to take you out to dinner?"

Sapphire shook her head. "No. I just wasn't prepared. I mean, I have to find clothes, do my nails, my hair."

"Sapphire, you have a clothing boutique in your closet, your nails are fine, and so is your hair. Like I said, it was a last-minute decision. Just roll with it and get ready."

Sapphire looked at Zeke as he stood with his arms folded across his chest. He wanted to take her to dinner. Excluding random dinner dates with other couples for business and occasionally for leisure, dining out was something they hadn't done in a while. She nodded her head. "OK."

Zeke forced a smile. "Thank you."

Sapphire folded the corner of the page she was reading, closed the book, and rose from her loveseat. "Where did you make the reservations?"

Zeke shrugged. "Just someplace someone recommended to me."

"Where? What type of food?"

"You'll see when we get there."

Sapphire smiled. She was enjoying the mystery. "Well, can you at least tell me how upscale the restaurant is?"

"It's just a small restaurant, baby. Nothing too exotic. You don't have to overdo it. Just look nice."

Sapphire walked over to Zeke, rose on to the tips of her toes, and draped her arms around his neck. "Nice, huh?"

Zeke wrapped his arms around her waist, and looked down at her. "Nice," he said.

Sapphire smiled. "I got your nice," she said, placing her lips on his.

For a split second, Zeke made a subtle move to pull away, but quickly reminded himself that he had to play his role and play it flawlessly. He tightened his hold around her and matched the intensity of her kiss, driving his tongue into her mouth.

Sapphire moaned and kissed him back feverishly. Zeke drove his tongue deeper and caressed her behind. Sapphire moaned louder, kissed him back harder, unclasped her hands from around his neck and went to his zipper and began to pull it down. Zeke squeezed her rear end harder and shivered from the feel of her touch as she removed his penis from his boxer briefs and began to stroke him.

Playing the role.

That's what he was doing.

Playing the role.

He wasn't truly enjoying the fire of their kiss. He wasn't in a state of near paralysis from her fingers moving back and forth around his now very erect and very thick shaft.

Playing the role.

He didn't miss the touch. His wife's touch. He didn't miss the passion. He was just going along with the plan he'd set in motion because she had fucked another man.

Another man.

Those two words hit him like a vicious blow to his midsection suddenly, and she stumbled back a step.

Sapphire looked up at him. "Are you OK?"

Zeke blinked several times and then looked at her. An image of her sitting atop her headless lover appeared in his head like camera flashes.

She'd fucked another man.

She'd . . . fucked . . . another . . . man.

Over and over, the statement repeated itself.

She'd fucked another man.

Play the role.

Zeke blinked again, then slid his quickly softening penis back into his boxers and zipped up his pants. "I'm fine," he said. "We just need to get a move on, that's all, or we're going to be late for our reservation."

Sapphire smiled seductively and stepped toward him. "Forget the dinner, Zeke," she said, reaching for his crotch again. "I'll cook something."

Zeke moved her hand away and stepped back. "Go and get dressed," he said, an edge in his tone. "I've heard a lot of good things about this place."

Sapphire was stunned. "We can go another time, Zeke," she insisted. "Dinner is not that important right now."

"I'm hungry," Zeke said. "You know how I don't function properly on an empty stomach."

Irritated, Sapphire snapped, "You *seemed* to be functioning just fine a second ago. Don't you want to make love to me?"

"Of course I want you, Sapph. That's a ridiculous question to ask."

"But—"

"I'm hungry, Sapphire. I want you in the worst way, but I've got to get some food in my stomach. Let's go and enjoy some time out together. I promise when we get back, I will more than make up for now."

Sapphire pouted. She wanted to protest again. She opened her mouth to do just that.

"I promise," Zeke said, before she could speak. "It will be well worth the wait."

Sapphire frowned and let out a sigh. "You promise?"

"I do."

Sapphire rolled her eyes. "OK. But it better be earth-shattering," she said with a smile.

Zeke gave her a smile, but didn't respond. Sapphire walked up to him, gave him a kiss on his lips, and said, "I love you, Zeke."

Zeke looked at her. Said, "I love you too."

Sapphire smiled, gave him another kiss, and went to get ready.

When she was out of view, Zeke closed his eyes tightly and pressed against his temples with the palms of his hands, as images of Sapphire and her adulterous acts ran through his mind in surround sound. He could hear her moaning and breathing heavily. Zeke pressed. Felt as though he could crush his own skull with both hands. Wanted to. Wanted to make the sounds stop. He clenched his jaws, stifled a moan. He was on the edge. Teetering, about to plummet. He breathed, squeezed, clenched, and told himself again:

Play the role.

Play the role.

Chapter 16

Thirty minutes later, whatever excitement Sapphire had been feeling drained from her body as Zeke parallel parked directly across the street from Tre's building.

Her heart beat like heavy drums as she sat silent and still.

Tre's apartment.

Right across the street.

The route Zeke had been taking had caused her some trepidation, but she let the anxious feeling go, surmising that she was just being paranoid. Sure, they were nearing Tre's neighborhood, but that didn't mean anything. But the closer they got, the heavier her heart beat, and the more she struggled to catch a breath. And when, instead of going past Tre's building, Zeke pulled to a stop across from it, Sapphire's heart all but stopped.

Tre's apartment.

Right across the street.

Coincidence?

She could barely catch a breath as she asked, "What . . . what are we doing here?"

Zeke gritted his teeth and looked over at his wife out of the corner of his eye. As Robin Thicke crooned, he'd glanced her way every once in a while during the drive, and as they'd gotten close, he'd seen her body become more and more tense. He tightened his hands around the steering wheel. He could practically smell her fear. It was as thick and strong as the floral perfume she had on.

He said, "The restaurant we're going to is a half a block down."

"What . . . what kind of food?"

"Japanese."

Sapphire's stomach turned. She looked past Zeke to Tre's building. "Why . . . are you parking here?"

"We're already close to missing our reservation. I didn't want to waste more time driving around trying to find a good parking spot." He looked at her intently. "Is something wrong?"

"Why don't . . ." She paused, cleared her throat, and started again. "Why don't you just use the valet parking?"

"Valet? Have you been here before?"

"N—no!" Sapphire stammered.

"How did you know they have valet?"

Sapphire cleared her throat again. "I . . . I just assumed I mean, most places have valet." She looked away from Zeke to Tre's building.

Zeke gritted his teeth. The smile was trying to force its way into existence again. He thought about the photos.

Sapphire riding.

Biting on her bottom lip.

Her headless lover.

Inside of her.

Making her moan.

Making her cum.

Zeke bore down again. Would break his teeth if he didn't ease up.

He said, "What's wrong?"

Sapphire put her focus back on him. "Nothing."

Zeke watched her as she wiped her palm of her hand, fiddled with the strap of her Coach bag, and then smoothed a crease on her dress. "Are you sure? You seem distracted."

Sapphire shook her head. "I'm fine."

"OK."

Sapphire exhaled. "It . . . it's just . . ." She paused, and looked back toward Tre's apartment.

Zeke watched her. The scent of her fear was stronger. "Yes?"

Sapphire exhaled again. "It's . . . well . . . Why don't you just do the valet?"

"Why? We have a good spot here. The restaurant's only a half a block away."

Sapphire wiped her forehead again. "This area . . ." She paused.

"Yeah?"

"It . . . it just doesn't seem safe to me."

"There's nothing wrong with this area, Sapph. People with money live here."

"That doesn't mean anything."

"This area is fine." Zeke cut the engine. "Come on. Let's get to the restaurant." He opened his car door and put one foot outside.

"Honestly, Zeke . . . I'm not really in the mood for Japanese."

Zeke turned and looked at her. "I heard the food is delicious."

"But—"

"Come on, Sapphire. Let's go and have some good food and enjoy each other's company."

Zeke watched her closely. She wanted to say no. She wanted to insist again that she wasn't in the mood for Japanese cuisine. But she couldn't say no and he knew it. Disgust formed a smile on his face. Watching her, being near her, loving and hating her at the same time—his stomach was in knots. The last thing he wanted was food, but he had to go through with the charade.

The role had to be played.

He had to hold on for a few more days. He had to be patient and endure the hurt. A few more days.

He leaned toward his wife, put a hand behind her neck, and pulled her toward him. His lips inches away from hers, smelling her perfume, her breath, he said, "I love you." He pressed his lips against hers softly and then pulled back. "Let's go and have a good time," he said.

He turned away and stepped out of the car.

Seconds later, Sapphire stepped out too.

Zeke took a breath of the evening air. *Play the role*, he thought. *Play the role.*

Chapter 17

"So, what do you think?"

Zeke stared at Sapphire. She was running her index finger slowly around the rim of her wine glass. "Sapphire?"

Sapphire looked up. She'd heard his question, but hadn't responded. She was trying her best to let go of the anxiety she was feeling. From the moment they'd walked into the restaurant, she couldn't ignore the ill feeling in her gut. She said, "Yes?"

"I asked what you thought of the place."

Sapphire picked up her glass and took a sip of her red wine. "I'm sorry, honey. The restaurant is very nice."

Zeke looked at her. *The look in his eyes*, Sapphire thought. Something about them made her uncomfortable.

"What? Why are you looking at me that way?"

Zeke shrugged. "You've hardly said a word since we got here. It just seems like something's bothering you."

Sapphire took another sip of her wine. "I . . . I'm fine. I'm sorry I've been so quiet. It may not seem like it, but I'm enjoying being here with you."

"Are you sure? I know this place isn't exactly what you're used to."

"I'm fine, really, Zeke." She reached across the table and put her hand in his. They'd been at the restaurant for twenty minutes. They'd ordered their food, gotten their drinks. So far everything had been OK. Perhaps everything would stay that way. The sick feeling in the pit of her stomach, the feeling that something was wrong, perhaps she'd caused that herself. She forced a smile on her face. She was out with her husband. This time together was something she'd been wanting. "I like the restaurant, Zeke. I was just thinking about some things."

"What things?"

"Nothing important."

"You sure?"

Sapphire nodded. "Yes, baby."

She smiled.

Zeke smiled back.

Silence took over.

Sapphire looked at her husband as he stared back at her with eyes devoid of the fire and intensity to which she'd been accustomed. The affection he was giving her seemed forced, and she couldn't help but wonder if he was sleeping around also. If that were the case, who'd begun the betrayal?

Had it been he, who, along with the hours spent away from home, had ultimately pushed her into the arms of a man willing to physically satisfy her so, that mentally she was able to continue a marriage in which she felt lonely?

Or had she been the one to cheat simply as a means of acquiring companionship that she hadn't gotten from her husband in a long time?

If that were so, could she really call what she'd been doing infidelity?

She said, "It's been a while since we've had time together like this."

Zeke nodded. "Yes, it has."

"I miss . . ." Sapphire paused mid-sentence as she caught sight of someone walking into the restaurant.

Tre.

With another woman.

Sapphire closed her mouth as her heart beat off rhythm. She tried not to stare as Tre and his date were escorted to a table off to the far corner of the room.

Her heart pounded.

Her palms became cold and sweaty as chills came over her.

Everything around her slowed down and disappeared one by one, until she was alone with Tre, his date, and her husband, who was calling her name.

Chapter 18

Zeke had seen the shock.
He'd heard her draw a breath.

He'd seen her body practically convulse.

He watched her staring, yet trying not to at the same time, as her world spun off of its axis.

He was there.

The headless man.

Zeke had had no idea if he frequented the restaurant, but he'd hoped that he did. At the very least, even if he didn't, Sapphire would be rattled just by being close to him with her husband.

His back facing the door, Zeke looked at his wife intensely, and seethed. He could have sat to Sapphire's right, or even directly beside her so that he too would have been able to see him, if by some slim chance he did come in. But he'd decided to sit facing his wife because he didn't want to see him. He was faceless in the photographs and faceless in his mind. Zeke wanted him to remain that way.

The images, the nightmares—they were bad enough without the face.

Zeke took a breath. Held it. Let the air sift and burn inside of his lungs.

He was there.

He exhaled and called his wife's name again. "Sapphire?"

Seconds passed before his wife looked at him. "Y . . . yes?"

Her eyes were wide. Her mouth hung open. She pulled her hand away, grabbed her glass, and swallowed the rest of her wine.

She'd tried to hide it, but Zeke had noticed the shake in her hand. "Are you OK?"

There was hesitation before Sapphire said, "Y—yes. I . . ." She paused, looked past Zeke momentarily, then focused back on him. "I . . . I want to go."

"Go? But our food hasn't come yet."

Sapphire shook her head. "I'm . . . I'm not feeling well."

"What's wrong?"

Another glance past him. This time her gaze remained focused there. "My . . . stomach's upset."

"All of a sudden?"

She looked back at him. "No. It . . . it was bothering me before, but I didn't want to say anything, but it's worse now."

"Is it gas? I'll grab the waiter and order a cup of tea. Maybe that will help."

Sapphire shook her head. "It's not gas."

"But—"

"Can we please go?" Sapphire said, her tone laced with anxiety.

Zeke stared at her for several seconds and then let out a sigh. "OK. Let me just get the waiter to box our food."

"I really don't want the food."

"But you may want to eat later."

Sapphire shook her head. "I won't."

"But—"

"I'm going to wait for you outside," she said, pushing her chair away from the table and standing up.

Before Zeke could say anything else, she started off toward the exit. Zeke turned and watched her walk. Head down. Purse clutched tightly in her hand.

He watched and waited.

One second.

Two seconds.

Three seconds.

At four, she slowed and looked ever so slightly to the right.

Zeke didn't follow her line of sight.

The headless man had to remain headless.

He waited until Sapphire quickened her pace a second later and hurried through the doors before removing three-hundred dollar bills from his wallet and leaving them beneath his glass. Hours before, he'd come to the restaurant and worked up a deal with the waiter.

Two hundred dollars for the best seat in the house.

The extra hundred was the tip.

Zeke stood up.

He thought about looking to the right to see him.

Thought about it.

Felt the muscles in his neck tense up.

He stood still.

Clenched his jaws.

Felt rage building inside of him.

His neck muscles were taut.

He took a breath.

The headless man. He had to stay fucking headless.

Zeke exhaled, letting out the air and rage slowly, and walked away from the table to leave the restaurant. Sapphire was already at the car waiting for him.

Tuesday—Three Days

Chapter 19

Sky—clear blue. Clouds—angelic white. The sun—bright yellow, spewing its rays in every direction, warming the air. Birds hovered, soared, glided, spoke amongst themselves chirping, squawking, singing sweet songs of desire, and carrying on conversations no one but they could understand. Planes flew high above them. People inside, seatbelts around their waists, listening to music coming from their iPods, while their neighbors read paperbacks or snored, or talked them to death.

They were all oblivious to the peace and tranquility beneath them. They had no clue about the amazement and beauty. They didn't understand the freedom.

But Tre did.

He understood, appreciated, and adored it because he was soaring in it. In the sky, amongst the clouds, within the intimate patterns the birds created.

He soared.

Did dips and dives, spiraled upward, and nose-dived.

With the wind in his face and blowing through his hair.
He soared.

His arms spread wide, through the cotton white, through
the rays of sunlight, speaking with the birds.

On his back, floating, he looked upward at the airplanes
above and felt sorry for the passengers confined in their
aisle, middle, and window seats. They didn't know the
peace he knew. They didn't know the calm.

The Zen.

Tre was meditating. Legs crisscrossed. Right ankle on
left knee. Left ankle on right knee. Elbows down at his
sides. Arms bent. Palms facing upward. Back straight.
Eyes closed.

The lotus position.

Mastered during his days in Japan, Tre found his center,
his calm, his Zen every morning before he began his day.
One hour in the sky. An escape from the world below. He
treasured this time. It was better than sleeping, because
when he found his Zen, his mind was at complete rest. No
dreams, no random nightmares. His mind was blank and
he was simply in the floating, existing, being.

One hour.

He needed no stopwatch or alarm clock to let him
know that his time was up because he was one with time;
mind, body, and soul.

One hour.

To avoid interruption, he turned off the ringer on the
house phone and kept his cell phone off. The rest of the
outside noise from beyond his windows would disappear
as he drew closer to his Zen.

Unfortunately, the incessant knocking coming from his
door was a sound that, no matter how hard he tried to ignore it, would not go away. Tre said good-bye to the birds,

glided down to the ground, and opened his eyes. The knocking had become a bang, accompanied with the sound of a familiar voice calling his name. He sighed, unfolded his legs, stood up, and went to open the door.

"Were you in on it?"

He hadn't even a chance to speak. He looked at Sapphire as though she'd lost her mind. "What?"

Sapphire stormed uninvited past him.

Tre sighed again, shook his head, closed the door, and turned around.

"Were you in on it?" Sapphire asked again. "Did you plot that together?"

Tre squinted his eyes and folded his arms across his sculpted, bare chest. "Sapphire . . . what the hell are you talking about?"

Sapphire ran her hand through her hair. "I'm talking about last night at the restaurant."

"The restaurant?"

"Yes!"

"You were there?"

Sapphire slit her eyes. "Like you didn't know."

"I didn't," Tre said matter-of-factly.

"You didn't see me?"

Tre shook his head. "No."

Sapphire formed a tight line with her lips and gave him an accusatory stare. "You didn't see me at all, huh?"

"No. I didn't."

Sapphire curled her lips. "Well, I saw you and your bitch."

Tre clenched his jaw. He'd seen this coming. Little by little the signs had become more obvious. The possessiveness. The showing up at his door unannounced. The casual, non business–related phone calls. The desire to see him more and more. The "friendly endearment" toward his other client.

Years ago, a client taught him all about the signs.

Lori Clark.

Mid-fifties, attractive, tanned, with a body like Maria Sharapova's. Lisa Clark. Her husband had been a stock market master who'd had a heart attack and died on the floor of the Stock Exchange. He'd left millions.

Lori began calling for Tre's services after learning from a friend of a friend of a friend that Tre had outstanding plumbing capabilities. Initially, she only called on Tre once, sometimes twice a month, to scratch her itch when needed. For the first three months of their arrangement, everything was fine. She paid Zeke handsomely, while Zeke gave her a great, no-holds-barred sexual experience each and every appointment.

But after three months, things began to change. Lisa started buying him gifts just because. She would call him during the week just to talk and to hear his voice. When she couldn't reach him by phone, she would just show up on his doorstep without warning. Tre had been naïve then. The gifts, the calls, the visits—he wrongfully assumed they were byproducts of the work he'd been doing in the bedroom. Each call, each gift, each visit had been a stroke to his ego. His dick was magic and he'd put Lisa under one hell of a spell.

That was how he'd felt until Lisa began going off on him in jealous tirades when he'd be unable to see her because of his obligations to other clients. That had been how he'd felt until Lisa began following him, often times disrupting his appointments. Tre began losing clients because of the drama Lisa caused, and would have lost them nodded and, without saying another word, walked out the door.

Tre didn't hesitate.

He closed the door behind her and went back to find his Zen.

He had other clients. Sapphire's money wouldn't be missed.

all, but luckily for him, she died in a head-on collision with a tractor-trailer. It had been a cold December mid-afternoon. The newspapers said she'd hydroplaned right into the truck and died instantly.

Tre shed no tears over her death. He'd been on the road on his way to see a client, and minutes before her accident, he'd seen her two car lengths behind him in his rear view mirror. He'd passed the semi when he increased his speed to lose her.

Tre was no longer naïve.

He ignored the bitch comment and asked, "Were you following me?"

Sapphire shook her head. "No."

"But you were at the restaurant."

"Because my husband took me there."

"I see."

"And he parked in front of your building."

"My building?"

"Yes." Sapphire ran her hands through her hair again, paced back and forth, and then sat down on his sofa. "Please tell me, Tre. Were you in on it?" Her face was a mask of fear and anxiety.

Tre shook his head. "No, Sapphire. I wasn't."

"Oh God," Sapphire whispered. "Then he has to know about us."

Tre raised an eyebrow. Lisa had liked to use the word "us" too. "Did he say something to you?"

"No."

Tre thought about the deal he'd made with Jewell. Fifteen thousand dollars to allow a photographer into his home to snap shots of Sapphire riding him. He had a set in his desk drawer at home. His head was cut off, as was the agreement between him and Jewell. He never asked, and didn't want to know, but he couldn't help but wonder now what Jewell had done with the pictures.

Had she shown them to her father? If so, with his head being cut off, the only way he would have known Tre's identity would have been for Jewell to have given him up.

They were at the restaurant, but he'd never been approached.

"Don't you think if your husband knew anything he would have said something?"

Sapphire exhaled heavily. "Maybe . . . I . . . I don't know."

Tre flared his nostrils. He wanted to get back to his meditating. "If I were married and I knew my wife was stepping out on me, I'd say something to her and I damn sure would say and do something to the other guy. I don't know many men that wouldn't. Is your husband the type of man to not do anything?"

Sapphire closed and opened her eyes slowly. "No," she said easily. "Knowing Zeke, he probably would have attacked you."

"Well . . . there you go."

"Unless you two arranged for that to take place."

"I don't play games like that."

"But—"

"Trust me, Sapphire . . . your husband and I have never spoken. His parking in front of my building, us being at the restaurant at the same time—that was just one hell of a coincidence. Had to be."

"How can you be so sure?"

"Because you're here without a mark on you and your husband never said a word to you or to me." He paused. "Where's your husband right now?"

"At work. He was gone before I woke up."

"Go home and relax, Sapphire."

"But . . . but what if he knows?"

"He doesn't know anything," Tre said. There was a lot of reassurance in his tone, but in the back of his mind, he couldn't help but wonder what Jewell's purpose had been with the photographs. "Go home," he said, walking to her and extending his hand to her.

Sapphire frowned, put her hand in his, and stood up. "I have a bad feeling, Tre."

"It's called a guilty conscience, Sapphire. Maybe you need to focus on fixing things with your husband."

Sapphire's shoulders sagged and her chin dropped down a notch.

Tre wasn't one to let go of easy money, but he had a bad feeling also. He'd said their being at the same restaurant had been a coincidence, but had it really? Again, he thought about the photographer in his closet. For the first time, he was regretting allowing the invasion of his privacy.

He escorted Sapphire to the door and opened it. It was time to let her go.

"Go home, Sapphire."

"Who was she, Tre? That woman . . . who was she?"

"She was a client, just like you."

"Is she . . . Does she mean anything?"

"Go home, Sapphire."

Sapphire looked at him. Her eyes were welling with tears. "Tre . . . I . . ."

"Go home," he said again.

Sapphire stared at him for a brief moment. By the expression on her face, his curt tone had surprised her. She

Chapter 20

He had to know.

That's all Sapphire kept thinking as she walked away from Tre's apartment. He may not have said anything, but she still couldn't help but feel that Zeke had to know.

Something.

He just had to.

Tre said it had been a coincidence, but Sapphire just couldn't believe that. Parking in front of Tre's building. Taking her to the Japanese restaurant.

A coincidence?

He didn't know anything, Tre had said. A guilty conscience. Could he have been right? Had Zeke been telling the truth? Had he simply parked there because they'd been running behind on the reservation and the spot had been convenient? He'd never once looked toward Tre's building. Wouldn't he have if he'd known or suspected something had been going on?

In the restaurant, Zeke had been calm, cool, normal. He

wanted to have dinner with his wife. Did a man who knew of his wife's infidelity behave that way? As though nothing were wrong. Could a man carry on as though everything were just fine? Could Zeke?

She'd seen him fly off the handle before. In his younger days he'd been something of a hothead. Quick on the draw sometimes, he would react before he thought. She saw those same qualities in Sam. Over the years, the lion inside of him learned to purr. If he'd known about her and Tre, Sapphire doubted the man she knew would remain quiet.

Did that mean Tre had been right?

Had it been her guilty conscience that had her on edge in the restaurant?

Zeke had never turned around when Tre and his "client" stepped inside. He never batted an eyelash or looked at her with a suspicious eye when she'd seen them walk in. During the drive home, he'd been nothing but worried about how she'd been feeling. When they arrived home, he'd been nothing but attentive, helping her change, propping up her pillows, fixing her a cup of tea. A man aware of his wife's betrayal wouldn't have done those things.

Tre had to be right.

Zeke had to have been totally oblivious.

Right?

Sapphire forced herself to take a deep breath as she reached the elevator. Focus on fixing things with Zeke. Tre's advice. She exhaled slowly and pressed the down button.

Zeke never said a word.

He'd only wanted dinner with his wife.

Focus on fixing things.

The elevator doors opened. Sapphire stepped inside.

"Hey! Hold the door!"

Sapphire turned. A young Latino, mid-twenties, was running down the hallway toward her.

Breathing heavily, he ran into the elevator. "Thanks," he said, standing beside her. "Waiting for the elevator is a bitch." He smiled.

Sapphire smiled back. "No problem." He was cordial, had a handsome smile, and seemed harmless, but Sapphire didn't like the vibe coming from him. She clutched her purse a little tighter.

"We must be on the same schedule."

Sapphire looked over at him. "Excuse me?"

"We rode the elevator together on the way up."

"Did we?"

"Yeah."

Sapphire said, "Oh."

He smiled. "Arriving and leaving at the same time. See . . . same schedule." He laughed.

As was his demeanor, it was a friendly, unassuming laugh. Still, Sapphire tightened her hold around her purse strap just a little more.

"You live here?" the Latino asked.

Sapphire shook her head. "No."

"Neither do I. I was visiting my girl before she goes to work. You?"

"Just a friend," Sapphire said curtly.

The elevator came to a stop as they reached the lobby. When the doors opened, he said, "Have a good day."

Sapphire gave him a polite smile. "Thank you. You too."

He smiled back, and for some reason, as amicable as he'd been, his smile gave Sapphire the chills. She stepped into the lobby and hurried outside, heading to her car.

Behind her, the Latino stood still outside of the apartment building's entrance and watched her. When Tre had opened his door for Sapphire, he'd been walking past, heading toward the end of the hallway. His assignment had been to follow Sapphire. To see if he could find out who her lover was. Neither Tre nor Sapphire had realized he'd been within earshot when she began to speak, and they had no idea that he'd been on the other side of the door eavesdropping on their conversation.

The Latino, whom Ty called Loc', which was short for "loco," watched Sapphire hurry away.

He and G were going to make an easy ten thousand apiece in a couple of days.

Thursday—One Day

Chapter 21

"Is everything ready?"

Zeke had just walked into Sam's office and closed the door.

Sam put down his pen and looked up at him. He clenched his jaws. "Everything's ready," he said.

Zeke nodded. "Good."

"Zeke . . . are you sure about this? I mean . . . we can go another route. This doesn't have to happen. I know what Sapphire's done hurts, but—"

"What would you do if Jewell allowed another man inside of her, Sam?" Zeke said, cutting him off. "What would you do if you saw her riding someone else's dick? If she were biting on her bottom lip because another man was moving back and forth inside of her pussy while you were at work?"

Sam tapped the index finger of his right hand on the desk as the visual of Zeke's words appeared in his mind. "I—"

"How would that make you feel, Sam? What would go through your mind? Would you wonder how long she'd been fucking him? Would you wonder if that other man's dick was covered with a condom? Or if it was inside of her raw and spilling cum?"

Sam tapped his finger harder and fidgeted in his seat. The visual—Jewell on top of someone else—was making his temperature rise.

"You were moving your dick inside of that intern, Sam. You were fucking her from behind as she bent over your desk. Can you imagine Jewell taking it that way? Can you see her moving back and forth to meet his thrusts? Can you hear her moaning, begging to be fucked harder, deeper? Can you hear her demanding for it faster?"

Sam flared his nostrils. Tapped his finger harder. Reached for his pen with his other hand, picked it up, and then put it back down. He'd fucked the intern hard, deep. He'd given it to her the way she'd wanted it. The way she'd demanded and begged for it.

The way he could now hear Jewell begging for it.

"Zeke . . ." He paused. Shook his head. Breathed in and out deeply. His heart beat heavily as his imagination worked involuntarily. His temperature rose by four more degrees.

Jewell fucking another man.

Riding him.

Taking it from behind.

"Would that 'hurt' you, Sam? If you received anonymous photographs? If someone else knew that Jewell was being an unfaithful whore? Would that 'hurt'? Would that kill you inside? Would you die over and over thinking about it? Seeing it in your fucking mind and then on photo paper that you can't make yourself throw away, but want to so badly? Would that make you cold? Make you fucking angry? Make you sad? Would that break you and make you hate?

"What would you do, Sam? How would you feel? Another man. Another man's dick."

Sam stopped tapping his finger and made fists with both hands as Zeke stared down at him. He clenched and unclenched his jaws furiously.

The image of Jewell doing to him what he'd done to her—it made his eyes burn. Until now, he thought he'd understood what Zeke had been going through. He thought he could understand the level of pain and anger. The magnitude of the hatred burning inside of him.

Until now.

He shook his head. Didn't speak. Just shook his head.

Zeke looked at him long and hard for a few seconds and then turned around and left the office. He didn't have to say anything else.

In his chair, Sam sat still, his hands in tight fists, the impact of his own actions, his own betrayal, hitting him hard.

"Christ," he whispered as tears snaked from the corners of his eyes. "What the fuck have I done?"

Chapter 22

Zeke sat in his car, his fingers gripping his steering wheel. Minutes earlier he'd been with Sam, painting a very vivid and clear picture of why there'd been no other route to take.

After the restaurant, playing the role had become increasingly more difficult. Being near Sapphire, touching her without strangling her—it had been hard.

So goddamned hard.

Tears fell from his eyes as he ground his teeth and choked the wheel. He moaned softly as Sapphire betrayed him in his mind again. As much as he loved her, he hated her now.

Never say never.

Nothing was impossible.

Two phrases he never thought there was any truth to, because he certainly never thought it would have been possible to love his wife any less than forever and a day, with his heart and soul. No relationship was ever perfect of course, and no one person was without her share of flaws, but the woman Sapphire was, or at least the woman he thought she was, had been perfect for him, and her perfect imperfections had given him a life he would always cherish.

But then the damn photographs arrived.

On laminated paper. 8x11. Pristine, clear, professional shots.

Sapphire wasn't an exhibitionist, but the show she performed, the expression she bore, the intensity she exuded—she clearly hadn't been let in on the photo shoot.

Zeke slammed his right hand down on the steering wheel. "Who the fuck are you?" he yelled. "Why did you send me the goddamned photos?"

Tears ran down his cheeks, as he wished for the power to go back in time. He wanted to be naïve again. He wanted to live life believing that his wife could and would never do him wrong. That she was a godsend sent to him for the sole purpose of completing him the way Renee Zellweger had completed Tom Cruise in *Jerry Maguire*. The way Jada completed Will.

He slammed his hand down on the wheel again. Did it over and over, each blow an imagined blow to Sapphire and her headless lover, to Sam and his intern, to the photographer and the photo paper used.

Over and over.

Each blow harder than the one before it.

"Why? Goddammit! Why?"

Tears fell harder now. Tears of pain. Tears of anger. Tears of disgust. Tears he'd been holding back.

Tears that held the last remaining portion of his sanity.

He hit the steering wheel again. The fabric of the control he'd had was being pulled away strand by strand.

Not now, he thought.

Not now.

"Not now!"

He was too close. He was almost there. He couldn't lose it now.

He hit the steering wheel again and shut his eyes tightly, forcing the salty tears to remain inside. He clenched his jaws, groaned, took air deep in his lungs.

Not now.

Not now.

He breathed. Focused. Breathed. Focused.

Not now . . . Not . . . now.

He opened his eyes, no longer having to worry about fresh tears, and wiped the old ones away with the back of his hand.

Not now.

He let the tension in his neck and shoulders ease away.

"Not now," he whispered.

When Sapphire was gone. When people would mistake his tears and his pain for grief. Then and only then could he let go.

When Sapphire was gone.

When the photographs could finally be thrown away.

But not now.

Now . . . he still had a role to play.

Zeke took one more deep breath, let it out slowly, and then slipped his key in the ignition and started the car.

Thirty minutes later, he was pulling into his driveway.

He sat still and stared at his home. He thought about the first time he and Sapphire had seen it. They'd been out with their realtor, Nancy. They'd been working with her for two weeks, searching for the perfect home. A few years before that day, they would never have dreamed that that type of search would be possible. They'd been struggling. Credit cards, student loans, rent, car—the bills were plenty and they'd been a steep mountain to climb. But then things took off with the company, and, little by little, the debt-to-cash ratio changed in their favor, and searching for their dream home just became the next obvious thing for them to do.

They'd fallen in love with the attention-grabbing, two-story turret from the moment they walked through the front door and stepped into a marbled foyer. A study was off to the right, dining room to the left, leading into the kitchen with breakfast area and sunken sunroom. The sunroom shared a see-through fireplace with the family room, where a bowed wall of windows allowed the sun to pour in. After taking a tour of the five bedrooms upstairs, they were sold. They put in a bid on the house, which was accepted, and two weeks later they were moving in.

It didn't take them long to make their new house a home, and before long, they were creating memories that would last forever. Memories that Zeke now wished would go away.

He sat silent, unmoving.

He'd sell the house two weeks after she was gone.

Another byproduct of the insanity posed as grief.

Being in the home with her not being there would be too hard. He needed new surroundings, a different environment. Something unfamiliar.

This is what he would tell everyone. This would be his reasoning.

Zeke turned off the car and pulled the keys out of the ignition. All he had to do was play for one more day.

The role of a lifetime.

He got out of the car, wanting to take his gun from the glove compartment with him, and went inside.

Chapter 23

"What's this?"

Vanilla-scented candles had been lit and spread throughout the room. "Bolero" played by Pink Martini, an ensemble band introduced to Sapphire by her friend Marlene, who'd been introduced to them by her associate, Lisette. They were a worldly band, fusing jazz, samba, and African rhythms, with Japanese, Spanish, and French lyrics sung beautifully by their lead singer, China Forbes.

Listening to Pink Martini was like being in a dimly lit lounge, painted in deep red tones, its walls covered with framed photographs of various celebrities from the past and present who'd all passed through to bless the establishment with smooth, sexy, entrancing, memorable performances. Etta James, Diana Krall, Will Downing, Najee. No food served, this was just the place to be to set up the romance before the passion.

Pink Martini had many songs to choose from, but Sapphire chose "Bolero" for its seductive sound, because seduction was the mood she wanted to create.

Candlelight, Pink Martini, and chilled wine.

Tre had said to focus on fixing things.

That had Zeke known anything, he would have said something.

It had been two days since the non-incident happened at the restaurant and Zeke still had not said a word.

Sapphire had been thinking about things seriously during those two days and had come to three conclusions. One: Tre was right—Zeke knew nothing. Or two: he was wrong. And if that was the case, then there was conclusion number three: in her mind, if he knew about her and Tre and hadn't said anything, that meant that she was not the only one guilty of infidelity.

Focus on fixing things.

That's just what she intended on doing.

She smiled seductively at her husband, who'd just walked into the bedroom. He looked tired. *Overworking himself as usual*, Sapphire thought.

She approached him with two wine glasses in her hand. "This," she said, handing him one, "is for you."

He took the glass and looked down at her, his expression unreadable. "For me?"

Sapphire kissed him sensually on his lips, and then backed away. "Yes." She took a sip of her wine and then put her glass down on the night table. "And so is this." She untied the terrycloth robe she'd been wearing and let it fall to the ground. She had nothing on but an open mesh chemise, courtesy of Frederick's of Hollywood.

She stood with her hands resting on her waist. She'd lived for fifty-four years, but her body was showing the wear and tear of a thirty-four-year-old. Keeping up her appearance had always been important to Sapphire. Running daily, swimming three times a week at the gym, doing yoga every morning, eating the right foods. Sapphire fully believed that her body was a temple to be preserved. That was one of the reasons Jewell was an only child. She didn't like the way her body had changed during the nine-month term. The weight gain, the way her nose spread, the swollen ankles, the stretch marks that she'd had covered up by plastic surgery. Before she left the hospital, she'd had her tubes tied.

Zeke was initially upset about her decision, because he did want to have at least one more child, but as Jewell grew and occupied his mind, time, and heart, his desire disappeared.

"Do you like?" Sapphire looked at Zeke. He was staring back at her, his mood still hard to detect by the look on his face. She did a full turn. "So?"

Zeke stared and remained silent. Sapphire called his name again, his silence making her uneasy, making her wonder which conclusion had been the right one.

"Zeke? Is something wrong?"

Zeke shook his head. "No. Why?"

"You haven't said anything. Does the outfit look that bad?"

Zeke shook his head again. "I wasn't expecting this. You just caught me off guard."

Sapphire smiled seductively. "Unexpected can be a good thing." She bit down on her bottom lip and sat on the bed. "Come here," she said, her voice as sultry as China Forbes's smooth staccato.

Zeke stood still for a moment and then downed his wine in one swallow. He put his empty glass on the dressing table and went to her.

"I want to suck on you, Zeke," Sapphire said, reaching up and grabbing hold of his belt. "I want to feel you grow inside of my mouth." She undid his belt and then unclasped his pants and pulled them, along with his boxer briefs, down. "You've always been built so nicely," she said, wrapping her fingers around his hardening shaft. "Your dick has always been so perfect."

She stroked him gently a few times and then took him into her mouth. She moaned as she sucked on him. Moaned as she ran her tongue up and down.

Zeke moaned from the magic of Sapphire's fellatio. He throbbed as she ran her tongue around the tip of his swollen head. He began to move his hips back and forth, fucking her mouth.

Sapphire welcomed the motion, covering his penis with more saliva, swallowing him deeper, trying to take him to the back of her throat.

Zeke moaned, throbbed again, and put his hands on the back of her head.

Sapphire felt his girth become thicker. A few more strokes and he would explode. A few more circles around his tip and she would taste him.

Zeke moaned louder.

Fucked her mouth harder.

Sapphire tightened her mouth. Felt his blood pumping on her lips.

He was almost there.

About to spill.

About to drown her with brothers and sisters for Jewell that could never be.

Sapphire sucked him one more time, and then let go and pulled back. She looked up at him. "Come and fuck me, Ezekiel." She moved back on the bed.

Zeke stepped out of his pants and briefs, which were gathered at his ankles, and climbed onto the bed with her.

Sapphire ran her hands over his toned chest, his ever-so-slight belly. His body, too, did not look its age.

"How do you want me, Zeke? How do you want me to take it?"

Zeke looked at her, an animalistic glint in his eyes. "Turn over."

Sapphire did, getting on her hands and knees. "Take it," she said. "Fuck me."

Zeke clenched his jaws and moved forward, grabbed her, pushed her chemise up, and slid himself inside of her.

Sapphire gasped from his thickness.

Zeke moved back and forth. Rammed his pelvis against her ass cheeks.

Sapphire took quick breaths from the intensity of his movement. He was taking it in a way he hadn't in a long while. Fucking her, hurting her. His tip pounded her insides. Her clit screamed from the friction.

"Oh shit, Zeke! Oh . . . shit . . . That . . . that hurts . . . shit . . . give . . . give it to . . . me."

She moved her hips back to meet him as he came forward, to meet the abuse he was administering. Her eyes watered with each thrust. Her pussy screamed, burned, begged for mercy, begged to be punished.

"Fuck . . . fuck me . . . Zeke. Fuck . . . fuck . . . fuck . . ."

"Who does this pussy belong to?" Zeke asked.

Sapphire breathed out. "It . . . it's yours."

Zeke pulled out to the tip and slammed back into her. "Whose?"

Tears fell from her eyes, the pain unbearable and incredible at the same time. "Yours."

Zeke pulled out. Drove back in. Deep. Hard. Unforgiving. "Whose is it?" he demanded again. His tone was guttural. Laced with vehemence.

Tears continued to fall harder. She wanted him to stop. The pain too intense. She cried as he drove himself into her again.

"Whose is it?"

He pounded her.

Sapphire couldn't take it anymore. She tried to pull away, but Zeke clamped his fingers around her waist, refusing to let her go. He moved back and forth.

Sapphire was crying now, her tears no longer a mixture of pleasure and pain. "P—please . . . I . . . I can't—"

Zeke continued to pound. "Whose goddamned pussy is this?" he yelled. "Whose?"

Sapphire screamed out. "Zeke! Please!"

"Whose! Whose is it?"

"Yours! It's . . . yours!"

Zeke let out a carnal scream, drove his dick into her with incredible force, and came.

Sapphire cried out as he exploded.

Zeke bucked several times and then unclamped his fingers from around her waist. He pulled out of her completely, and without a word, got off of the bed, grabbed his pants and shoes, went into the bathroom, and slammed the door shut.

On the bed, Sapphire collapsed forward and buried her face in her pillow. She cried hard, body-trembling tears as her vagina throbbed. *Not my husband*, she thought. The cum leaking out of her did not belong to her husband. She curled into a fetal position. Her husband would have never done that. He was always gentle, always considerate, making sure that she released first. He would have never fucked her that way.

Sapphire's body shook.

Her tears fell in rivers.

That wasn't her husband.

She cried.

She hurt.

She shook.

And she realized right then and there that Tre had been wrong and she'd been right.

He knew.

Chapter 24

Zeke gripped the edge of the sink and stared into the mirror. Eyes, red and filled with malicious intent. Jaw clenched, teeth bared, nostrils flared: he didn't recognize the person staring back at him.

He stared, breathed heavily as though he'd been running one-hundred-yard dash sprints over and over.

Sapphire was on the bed crying.

He stared. He listened. He'd almost lost it. Almost wrapped his fingers around her throat, strangled and fucked her at the same time.

Almost.

He wanted to so bad. He wanted to hurt, punish, and then kill her.

Whose pussy?

It was supposed to have been only his. That's what the vows meant.

His pussy for better or for worse. His pussy through sickness and health. His pussy 'til death did they part.

But it wasn't.

Goddamn it, it wasn't.

It belonged to him now.

The headless lover. The man whose face he would never be able to recognize, yet would never forget. His wife's pussy was his now. Her betrayal was her divorce and her second marriage at the same time.

It fucking belonged to him now.

Sapphire cried.

The sound of her made Zeke's head hurt.

He looked at the monster in the mirror. Whispered, "Fuck you. Fuck you."

He shook the sides of the sink. Tried to rip it from its base. Sapphire's sobbing continued to administer sharp jabs to his temples.

He hated her.

He hated the headless man.

He hated Sam.

Hate consumed him.

Hate stared back at him with a devilish grin.

The man he used to be was no more.

Hate had killed him.

Zeke clenched his jaws harder. Felt what remaining bits of his heart he had left shatter, and turned away from the mirror.

Betrayal.

The word stung at his core like shards of jagged glass cutting into his skin. It burned like vinegar being poured into those cuts.

Betrayal.

Zeke slid into his briefs, put on his pants, slid his feet into his shoes. He turned and looked back at the monster in the mirror. "Fuck you," he said again. He spat in the monster's face and then turned around, opened the bathroom door, and walked out of the bedroom, leaving his wife behind.

For good.

Friday—The Day

Chapter 25

"Jewell . . . have you seen or spoken to your father today?"

Jewell breathed out heavily, regretting having picked up the phone. She'd been sleeping when the phone rang. She hadn't been feeling that well. For a little over a week, she'd been feeling tired, run down. Before the call, she'd been dreaming about random things. Dinner with the Obamas in the White House. Dancing at a concert with Robin Thicke and John Legend. Giving a speech at a nursing home, wearing nothing but lingerie. Random dream segments that made no sense at all. In one of the dreams the phone started to ring. She thought she'd been dreaming when she answered.

"Dad? No, I haven't. Why?"

There was a long pause before her mother responded. "I . . . I was just wondering." She sniffled a couple of times.

Jewell sat up. Was her mother crying?

She thought about the photographs and looked toward her closet. Her copies were there, hidden inside of a purse tucked away in the back. "Is everything OK?"

Her mother cleared her throat. "Everything is fine, Jewell. Everything is just fine."

"Is Dad OK?"

Her mother breathed heavily into the phone. "Always about your father," she said.

"What?"

"I said . . . it's always about your father, Jewell. He's the only person you ever seem to be concerned about. I realize you never really loved me, but couldn't you have at least cared a little? Just once it would be nice to hear you ask about me, about how I'm feeling."

Jewell sighed. "Mom, look, I'm not really in the mood right now."

"Of course you're not, Jewell. But I bet if your goddamned father were on the phone instead of me, you'd be just fine."

Jewell closed her eyes and tilted her head back. She'd held her tongue before, but if her mother didn't leave her alone . . .

"All I did was ask if Dad was OK," she said, doing her best to remain calm.

"Yes, yes," her mother snapped. "Your father, Mr. Perfect. Mr. Wonderful."

"Mom—" Jewell started.

"As much as you think he is, your father's not perfect, you know."

Jewell shook her head and slammed her fist down on the mattress. *How dare she! How dare she go there!*

"So what, Mom, you are? You're Mrs. Wonderful?"

"I never said that."

"And you know what? You better never say that!"

"Jewell, what—"

Jewell had been trying to hold it back, but couldn't any longer. Her mother had gone there and she couldn't hold her tongue any longer.

"You're a liar, Mom. A liar and an ungrateful bitch!"

"Excuse me?"

"Excuse you? There *is* no excuse for you!"

"Jewell, I think you better—"

"I don't give a damn what you think!"

"Jewell!"

"Just tell me: how could you? How could you betray Dad? After all he's done, how could you whore around and spend Dad's hard earned money on a fucking gigolo?"

There was silence for a few seconds before Sapphire said, "H—how . . . how did you know?"

"I saw you with him! I saw you kissing him! And you know what? I spoke to him too, and he told me all about the special services he provides to you."

"Jewell . . . let me explain—"

"I don't want your explanations, Mom! You have the nerve to complain about Dad not being perfect, you have the audacity . . . A gigolo! You're disgusting! You don't deserve to be with a man like Dad. I'm so glad I sent him those pictures, so he could see what a slut you really are!"

"Pictures? Pictures of what?"

"Of you fucking your male whore!"

"How . . . how did you—"

Jewell scoffed. "Your gigolo. I paid him to allow a photographer to hide out in his closet so he could take pictures of you two together."

"Jewell . . . no!"

"I have copies. Your gigolo has copies and I sent Dad copies anonymously!"

"No, Jewell! No! No!" her mother yelled out.

"Yes, Mom!"

"How could you?"

"How could I? How could you? Dad was always there."

"For you, Jewell! He's always there for you! But not always for me! Oh God! What have you done?"

"I've freed Dad, that's what I've done. I hope he threw those photos right in your face!"

"He . . . he never showed me the photos."

"What do you mean he never showed them to you?"

"He never showed me the goddamned photographs, Jewell! He never mentioned them. Oh God! I . . . I have to go. I need to find him."

Sapphire hung up the phone.

Jewell sat still with the phone clenched in her hand, breathing heavily. Her heart thudded in her chest. Her hand trembled with anxiety.

He hadn't shown her the photographs.

He hadn't mentioned them.

What had he done with them?

She was positive he'd gotten them, because she'd put them on his desk herself.

Had someone gone in his office and taken them?

No. She was sure he had them.

So what happened?

Jewell clicked the talk button on the phone and dialed her father's cell number. He always answered when she called.

The phone rang. And rang. And rang. And then went to his voice mail.

"Dad, call me, please! I need to speak to you. I love you."

She hung up, then dialed his office number. She ended up leaving the exact same message there.

"Where are you?"

She had a bad feeling. A twisting in the pit of her stomach. She clicked the talk button and dialed Sam's cell phone. It, too, went to voice mail. She didn't leave a message.

She got up from the bed, the knotting in her stomach worsening. She had to find her father and talk to him. She started toward the closet to grab some clothes, when she suddenly retched. She put her hand over her mouth and ran quickly into the bathroom, making it just in time to throw up in front of the toilet.

Chapter 26

"Jewell!"

Sam had just come home from work and walked into the bathroom to see her dry heaving into the toilet bowl. Vomit lay on the floor and in the front and inside of the toilet bowl.

Sam avoided stepping in the mess on the floor and stood above Jewell, putting his hand on the small of her back.

"Jewell . . . are you OK?"

Jewell dry heaved again, then coughed, spat, and nodded. "I . . . I'm OK."

Sam helped her stand up and go to the sink. She turned on the cold water, washed out her mouth, and wiped off her face.

"What happened?" Sam asked.

Jewell turned off the water, shook her head, and shrugged. "I don't know. One minute I was on the phone arguing with my mother, and the next thing I know, my stomach turned."

"Arguing with your mother? Is everything OK?"

Jewell kept her head down and didn't respond.

"Jewell? Is everything OK with your mom?" Sam asked again, her silence unsettling him. Jewell turned around and looked up at him. Something in her expression troubled him, made him wary. "Jewell, what happened with your mom?"

Jewell gave him a forlorn look. "Did you see my father at work today?"

Sam shook his head. "No." He hadn't seen Zeke since the day before.

"Did you talk to him at all today?"

Again, Sam shook his head. "No."

"I need to speak to him," Jewell said, going into the bedroom. She went to the bed, grabbed the phone, dialed her father's number and then hung up a few seconds later. She went to her closet.

Sam stepped out of the bedroom. The panic in her voice, the frantic pace in which she moved around worried him. There wasn't supposed to be anxiety in her voice yet. He'd been dreading that moment. Dreading the sight of the emotional turmoil she was going to have to endure. Her pain was a necessary evil.

He'd taken her out the night before to prepare her for what was to come. Dinner, movies, dancing, passionate sex in the middle of the night. Things had been strained for a few days between them, and he wanted that mood changed. The things she was about to go through emotionally . . . Taking her out, making her smile, laugh, pleasing her physically, this was his way of reminding her that he was there for her. He needed for her to be reassured of that, because she was going to need him like never before.

"Jewell, what's wrong? Don't you think you should lie down?"

Jewell grabbed a pair of Mavi jeans and a light blue sweater turned inside out. "I . . . I need to find my father."

Sam went to his wife as she turned away from the closet. Tears were falling from her eyes.

"Why are you crying?"

Jewell looked up at him. Her bottom lip was quivering. Sam enveloped her in his arms. "What's wrong?" he asked again as she trembled against him. His heart began beating heavily.

"I . . . I did something, Sam."

Sam kissed her on the top of her head and inhaled her Herbal Essences shampoo. "What, baby? What did you do? Talk to me."

Jewell cried, trembled.

Sam's heart beat harder, faster.

He hadn't been bitten by a radioactive spider, and he couldn't climb walls or fire webs from his wrists, but his spider sense was tingling like crazy. "Talk to me," he said again. "What happened between you and your mother? Why do you need to find Zeke so badly?"

"A . . . a few weeks ago, I saw my mother with . . . with another man. They were at a restaurant. She was kissing him."

Sam's heart beat skipped a beat. The tingling of his spider sense, warning him of danger, increased in intensity. He looked down at the top of Jewell's head. "What did you do, Jewell?" he asked, his tone ominous.

Jewell sniffled. "I waited until my mother left, and then I . . . I . . ." She paused.

"You what?"

"I approached the man. I spoke to him. He's a gigolo, Sam. A goddamned gigolo. Can you believe it?"

"What did you do, Jewell?"

Sam barely breathed as his heart rate increased.

"I . . . I paid him . . ." She paused, took a breath.

Sam closed his eyes slowly and released an oh-shit-filled sighed. He grabbed Jewell by her arms and held her out in front of him. "What did you pay him to do?"

Jewell looked up at him. "Sam, what's wrong? Why are you looking at me like that?"

"What did you pay him to do, Jewell?" Sam asked again, ignoring her questions.

"I paid him to . . . to have pictures taken."

Sam's heart fell into the pit of his stomach.

He let go of his wife's arms, backed away a couple of steps, and clamped his right hand down over the back of his neck. "Oh, Christ," he said. He looked at Jewell, who was looking back at him, confused. "What were the pictures of?"

"Sam? What . . . what's wrong?"

"Just tell me what the fucking pictures were of."

"Sam?"

"What were the fucking pictures of, Jewell!" he yelled.

Jewell jumped a bit, his outburst shocking her. "They were pictures of them . . . together."

"Of them together? Of who together?"

"My mother and her gigolo."

"Doing what?"

"Having sex."

Sam squeezed the back of his neck, paced around, let go of his neck, squeezed his temples with his thumb and middle finger. "Oh Christ," he said, the entire time. "Christ! Christ!"

"Sam?"

Sam looked at her. "What did you do with the photos?"

"Sam . . . what's wrong?"

"The photos!" Sam yelled. "What did you do with them?"

Tears fell down Jewell's cheeks. "I had copies made. For me, the gigolo, and . . . and for Dad."

Sam paced. Dragged his hand down over his face. "Shit! Shit!"

She knew.

She'd had the pictures taken.

She'd sent them.

Everything that was happening.

She'd been the catalyst.

"Shit!"

It would all happen soon.

"Shit!" he said again. He looked at his wife. Shook his head. "You have no idea what you've done, Jewell!"

"What? What do you mean?"

Sam paced. "You have no fucking idea what you've done!"

He dragged his hand down his face again.

Soon Ty would have Loc' and G pay a visit to Sapphire and her lover. Soon they would both be dead.

He looked at his watch.

"Goddammit, Jewell! What the fuck have you done?"

Sam ran out of the room.

Jewell called out his name, yelled for him to stop.

Sam ignored her.

He raced out of the house, hurried to his car, started the engine, and sped out of the driveway.

He grabbed his cell. Was about to make a call when it rang.

Jewell.

"Shit!" he screamed.

He pressed ignore and dialed Ty's cell number.

He was going 50 mph in a 30-mph zone as Ron Browz's single "Pop Champagne" went off in his ear, until Ty answered.

"'Sup, nigga. You got the other half of my money?"

Sam had given him half during their first meeting. Ty and his boys weren't going to get the rest until the job had been completed. Random home invasions, that's how the killings were supposed to look.

Sam said, "Ty, man . . . we gotta call this off!"

"Call it off? Nigga, shit's already in motion."

"Shit! Ty, man . . . call your boys. Tell them it's off. You'll still get your money!"

"Sorry, nigga, but I can't do that. They ain't roll with no cell phones. They went clean with no chance to leave shit behind."

"Shit! Shit!" Sam yelled as he ran a red light.

"A deal is a deal, nigga. You know how I do. There ain't no callin' shit off."

"Shit!"

"Don't fuck wit' my money, nigga. You fuck with my money and we'll be payin' yo' ass a visit."

Ty ended the call.

Sam cursed again and then dialed Zeke's cell.

It rang once and then Zeke answered. "Can I come home?"

"Zeke, listen—"

"Can I come home, Sam?" Zeke asked again, cutting him off.

"No! But—"

"Then why are you calling me?"

"Zeke—"

"Don't call me until it's done and I can come home."
Zeke ended the call.

Sam hit his steering wheel. "Shit! You've got to be fucking kidding me!" He dialed Zeke's cell again. The call went unanswered this time. Sam cursed again and then dialed Sapphire's cell phone. He had to warn her. She had to get out of the house.

Her cell rang and went to voice mail.

"Sapphire . . . please . . . if you get this . . . please get out of the house! Please! Some guys are coming there to hurt you. You've got to get out of there now! Please!"

He ended the call, dialed Sapphire and Zeke's house number, and thought about leaving a message, but decided against it. The police would check the answering machine. He slammed his phone down on the passenger seat.

"Fuck!"

He pressed down hard on the brake and fishtailed as he made a U-turn. He was forty-five minutes away from Zeke's house.

He slammed down on the gas pedal and raced toward the highway.

His cell phone rang.

He looked at it.

Jewell again.

He ignored it and kept driving.

Chapter 27

Not again.
Tre sighed.

He was on his couch, playing a game of Madden '09 on his Xbox 360. His team, the New York Giants, were ahead by four touchdowns in the third quarter against the Dallas Cowboys. He hated the Cowboys. Hated T.O. Picking him up was the best thing they could have ever done as far as Tre was concerned. T.O. was like a virus. Inject him into the program and the whole system went bad. Tre was murdering T.O., intercepting every pass thrown his way.

He was playing the full regular season. Going for another Super Bowl. After the game he would switch over and join his friends online to play *Gears of War 2*. Friday nights were his night. He never took a client on this night. It was just him on his couch and a couple of friends he still kept in contact with on theirs. Some were in Texas, others in Maryland, one was even in Japan. On Friday nights they'd play and talk shit with their headsets on until one, two, sometimes three in the morning. No money spent. No female drama. It was the ultimate guys' night out.

Tre paused the game, put the controller down, and went to the door. He thought about his past client and the accident that had gotten her off of his back. He wasn't wishing for the same thing to happen now, but he damn sure didn't want the same bullshit. He thought he'd made things very clear the last time. His services were no longer available, not to her.

He stood by the door, shook his head, and wished he could make Sapphire and her banging on his door go the fuck away.

He opened the door. He was about to tell her to leave when he was smacked hard across his face.

"You son of a bitch!" Sapphire smacked him again. "You son of a bitch! How could you do that?"

She raised her hand to slap him again. Tre grabbed her by the wrist before she could.

"You goddamned asshole!"

Tre ran his tongue along the inside of his left cheek, the one she'd hit. Now he knew what Jewell had done with the pictures. He said, "So I guess the restaurant hadn't been a coincidence."

"You asshole!"

Sapphire tried to pull her hand away to slap him again, but Tre's grip was solid. She made an attempt with her other hand. Tre grabbed that too.

"Cut the shit, Sapphire," he said, his voice low, calm, and very stern.

Sapphire called him an "Asshole!" again and pulled her hands away.

"How, Tre? How could you do that to me? I was paying you. How could you take her money over mine?"

Tre folded his arms across his chest. "She was paying more," he said easily.

Sapphire's eyes widened and her mouth fell open slightly. His callous words had been a retaliatory slap. "You jerk. I thought we—"

"Shut the fuck up, Sapphire. There is no 'we.' I'm a fucking gigolo. You paid me to fuck you. Your daughter paid me more to fuck you. End of goddamned story."

Tears ran down Sapphire's face.

They meant nothing to Tre.

"You're a piece of shit, Tre! A trifling piece of shit!"

Tre nodded. "Yeah, but you never screamed that when I was in that pussy of yours."

"Asshole!" Sapphire tried to smack him and again he caught her by her wrist, only this time after grabbing hold of her with one hand, he took the other, grabbed her by her throat and spun her and slammed her back against the door. Sapphire cried out.

Tre glared at her. "Our arrangement is over, Sapphire."

She sobbed. "Don't you even care?"

Tre shook his head. "No. I don't."

"I can't believe I ever got involved with you."

Tre laughed. "It was never me you got involved with. It was only my dick."

"Fuck you!" Sapphire spat in his face.

Tre clenched his jaws, and tightened his grip around her neck. Respect is very important in the Japanese culture. He hated being disrespected. "You have to pay me if you want to do that. You know the rules."

Sapphire cursed him again.

Tre laughed and then pushed her into the middle of the hallway. "Go and deal with your dysfunctional family, Sapphire. And don't come back here anymore." He stepped back into his apartment and slammed the door shut.

Sapphire cursed him out from the hallway.

He stood still for a moment and waited. A few seconds later, he heard Sapphire crying as she shuffled away from the door.

He took a breath, held it in, then released it slowly. He went back to the couch and looked at the time on his cable box. "Damn," he said. He'd be at least a half hour behind meeting the guys online by the time he finished his discarding of the Cowboys, to be 6-0 for the season.

He grabbed his controller, restarted the game, and ran a quick slant route to Kevin Boss for eleven yards. He ran another play, a run up the middle with Brandon Jacobs. He gained four yards on that play. He threw another quick strike for four yards to Steve Smith. "Yeah, baby!"

Third and two.

He'd get Derrick Ward to bounce to the outside for that one, maybe even break it for a touchdown run.

He chose the play.

Hit the right button to fake the hike, trying to draw the Cowboys offsides. They didn't bite. It didn't matter.

His thumb was about to press down on the A button to snap the ball, when a knocking came from the door again.

"Goddamn."

He paused the game and slammed the controller down so hard it bounced from the sofa to the floor. "Fucking bitch." He stood up and went to the door. This would be the last time she'd bother him.

He pulled the door open.

Before he could speak, someone wearing all black, with a ski mask revealing only a pair of steel-grey eyes, plunged a knife deep into his belly. Once, twice, and then a third time.

Tre gasped as his midsection stung. He looked down at the blade stuck inside of him, and then up at his assailant, who immediately hit him hard in the face. His nose broken, and blood flowing, he grunted and fell hard to the ground onto his back.

His attacker slammed the door shut, rushed and kicked him, and then bent down and stabbed Tre again in his stomach and side.

Tre rolled over and tried to crawl away from his attacker, who was standing, watching him.

He gasped for air.

Everything around him was spinning.

He coughed up blood.

Felt his body burn.

He crawled.

Toward his controller.

He hadn't meant to let it fall to the hardwood floor. Something like that could make the controller defective.

He gasped again.

Wheezed.

Blood bubbled from his broken nostrils.

Without question, he was dying.

Who was his attacker? Why was he there?

Tre wanted to ask, but couldn't find the strength to speak.

He crawled, the controller so close, yet so far away, but before he could reach it, his attacker stepped past him, picked it up, and sat down on the couch.

Tre gasped again.

Everything was fading.

He was getting cold.

Death was about to claim him.

Whenever people came close to death, they always mentioned how their whole lives flashed before their eyes. *Bullshit*, he thought. He wasn't thinking about his whole life as his world became black.

As his attacker restarted the game and the crowd roared, Tre wondered if Derrick Ward would get the first down.

Chapter 28

Jewell couldn't sit still.

What had she done?

Sam's words repeated themselves over and over again. What had she done?

She tried calling Sam again. No answer.

She tried her father. No answer.

She tried her mother's cell. Again, no answer.

Jewell ran her hand through her hair, and again wondered what she had done.

She needed answers.

She threw on her Mavi jeans, her sweater.

She retched. She ran to the bathroom. Made it this time to dry heave into the toilet she still hadn't cleaned. She'd had steak the night before. That would be the last time for a while.

She washed out her mouth and went slowly back into the bedroom. Her body felt fatigued, her stomach queasy. She wanted to lie down so badly. But she couldn't.

She had to know what it was that she had done. What it was that made Sam run out of the house and ignore her calls. She grabbed her purse, went downstairs, grabbed her car keys, and then went to the car.

Her mother.

The last person to speak to her father.

She had to know something.

Jewell pulled out of the driveway, sleep and a toilet beckoning her. Neither would be pacified.

Chapter 29

Sam. Jewell. Sapphire.
Calls from all of them.

Sapphire's constant calls meant Sam still hadn't made things happen. He wouldn't answer Sam's calls until Sapphire's ceased completely.

As for Jewell's calls. Having Sapphire killed was going to please and satisfy him, but her death was going to hurt his little girl. He didn't want to have to deal with that on his mind until everything was done. So he refused to take hers, too.

He downed the rest of the Jack and Coke he had sitting in front of him, and made motion to the bartender for another.

He was in Virginia Beach at the Marriott.

He'd had a meeting a few hours earlier. The meeting had been unplanned. An emergency meeting to take care of an emergency situation. It started at eight in the morning and went until six in the evening. He'd booked the hotel and driven in the night before, because he wanted to get a decent amount of sleep. He was supposed to drive back home afterward, but he was exhausted, so he decided to stay an extra night and leave in the morning.

That was his alibi.

He had purpose. He had witnesses.

The bartender brought him another glass. He looked at the bartender. Female. Latina. Looked like a thirty-something Rita Moreno. He'd never dated a Latina. He'd always found Latinas attractive, but he'd never made an attempt to date one, not because he couldn't catch their eyes, but because he didn't have the moves. He grew up listening to Motown and seventies funk. He had learned and mastered the Grind, the Hustle, the Electric Slide. He never listened to Salsa, Merengue, or any other type of Latin music. To be with a Latina—a real Latina—you had to have the moves. Zeke had the moves now. Something he'd acquired as he'd gotten older. But he was married. At least until her phone calls stopped coming in.

He gave the bartender a smile. She reciprocated, revealing deep dimples. Zeke took a look down at her ring finger, saw that it was naked, and thought about coming back after the dust settled. He said, "Bring me two more, please."

The bartender showed her deep dimples again, and said, "No problem."

"Bad day?"

Zeke looked to his right. Two stools down, an attractive brunette, her hair pinned up, was looking in his direction. Zeke stared at her. She was casually sexy in a red sweater that slouched at the neck and hugged a slender torso, accentuating a pair of full breasts, and a pair of dark blue jeans that fit like a second layer of skin. Black stilettos on her feet set her look off.

Zeke nodded. "Frustrating day."

The brunette smiled. "Those are worse than bad days."

"How so?"

"A bad day is just bad. It can't really be fixed. You just suffer through it and wait for the next day to come. When a day's frustrating, it means there are opportunities to set things right, but for whatever reason, something goes wrong to keep that from happening. Frustrating is peaks and valleys. You fall downhill and then climb back up a few feet, before you fall again. Bad is just falling down the hill until you mercifully hit the bottom and break your crown."

Zeke raised an eyebrow. "I never looked at it that way. I just always thought they were one and the same."

"Most people don't."

Zeke nodded again and then looked the brunette up and down. She was Kate Hudson attractive, but with the three Jack and Cokes in his system, each one stronger than the next, she was looking more like Scarlett Johansson. The bartender brought his two additional glasses. He asked, "Drinking alone?"

"I am. Are you?"

"If you slide down one stool then no, I'm not."

The brunette smiled seductively, then got up and moved down.

Zeke offered his hand. "Zeke."

The brunette took it. "Leah."

"Nice to meet you, Leah."

"Very nice to meet you, Zeke."

"Hadn't noticed you over there. Thought I was alone."

"I came fifteen minutes after you. You were deep in

thought. The building could have been on fire and I don't think you would have noticed."

Zeke shrugged. "Very frustrating day," he said.

"Hope it's getting better."

"It is."

"I'm glad."

Zeke smiled. "So what are you drinking?"

"Sex on the beach."

"Beach is closed isn't it?"

"You can still have sex, though."

Zeke laughed.

Leah did too.

The sexual energy was high.

Zeke ordered Leah's drink.

"So why are you here, Zeke?" Leah asked.

"Business. And you?"

"Visiting a friend."

"And where is your friend now?"

"Working. He's a doctor. Got called in to surgery. He'll be there until tomorrow."

Zeke nodded, swallowed one of the drinks and picked up the other. As he did, his cell phone vibrated. He looked down at it.

Sapphire.

Still.

He clenched his jaws.

"Bad call?" Leah asked.

"Very bad call."

Rita Moreno's lookalike brought Leah's drink. Leah thanked her, took a sip, then said, "Wife?"

Zeke passed his thumb over his wedding band. He wanted to take it off, but he had to be patient. He said, "Wife."

"Turning your frustrating day into a bad one?"

"Very much so."

His phone vibrated again.

Sapphire.

Again.

He put his phone on silent and slid it into his pocket.

"Seems like you could really use a stress relief," Leah said easily.

Zeke chuckled. "A neck and back massage."

"What about the rest of you?"

Zeke looked at Leah. She was staring back at him, her eyes lustful. She licked her lips.

Zeke said, "That, too."

"I give one hell of a fabulous full-body massage."

Zeke closed his eyes a bit. "Free of charge?"

"I'm not a prostitute if that's what you're asking."

"Was wondering."

"You're an attractive man, Zeke."

"You're very sexy, Leah."

"My friend is attractive, too, but he's not here."

"His loss."

"We're adults, are we not, Zeke?"

Zeke gave her a nod. "We are."

"I'm not looking for anything."

"Neither am I."

"But sex on the beach would be nice."

"Too cold for the beach."

"Your room would do."

Zeke stared at her, the alcohol and Sapphire's constant calling making him warm inside. He pulled out his wallet, placed three twenties on the bar counter, stood up and held out his hand for Leah to take.

*   *   *

Ten minutes later, Leah was straddled on top of Zeke. Her back was facing him, the way Sapphire's back had been facing her headless lover.

Zeke thrust upward, the way the headless man had.

Leah moaned, pushed down, and ground her hips.

Zeke imagined her biting down on her lip. Like Sapphire. He said, "Grab your breasts. Squeeze your nipples. Lick them."

Leah let out a soft moan. "Let me turn around so you can see."

"No. Stay just the way you are."

He didn't need to see.

"I have pictures."

"Pictures?"

"In my mind. I can see. Just do it."

Zeke drove himself deep.

Leah moaned and did as she'd been ordered.

Zeke watched her, seeing not her, but his wife. Sucking on her breasts, running her tongue around her erect nipple.

Leah's arm became Sapphire's. Her white skin changed to a dark honey hue. Her brown hair became black.

Zeke's upper body morphed. Became younger, hairless, more sculpted.

He was a voyeur, watching the scene unfold.

Hearing it happen.

Smelling the sweaty odor of sex.

Sapphire pushed down, took her lover in as deeply as she could. She cursed, called out her lover's name. Told him not to stop. To give it to her. To release his stress.

Zeke's heart thudded as the sex took place.

He wanted to feel his fingers wrap themselves around Sapphire's neck, fuck and squeeze at the same time.

He watched. Ground his teeth together. Sweated. Struggled to breathe.

"That's right," Sapphire said. "Choke me, baby. Choke me. Give me that dick and squeeze! Oh yes!"

Zeke watched.

Felt it.

Smelled it.

Sapphire's body.

Sapphire's scent.

Without a head, the headless man growled. He was nearing the point, about to explode. He thrust his dick deeper, Sapphire's wetness making bumps rise from his skin.

With each moment of Sapphire's betrayal, Zeke's heart broke more and more. He hated her. He wanted her out of his life. He wanted her to stop calling.

The headless man's torso morphed back into his own. Leah stopped impersonating Sapphire. His hands around Leah's throat, he came. Hard. A tidal wave of semen spilled into his condom.

Leah leaned her head back and let out a cry as she erupted. When her orgasm passed, she turned her head and looked at Zeke over her shoulder. She smiled, and then without saying anything, climbed off of him, gathered her clothes, and went into the bathroom. She showered and came out a few minutes later, looking as though she'd never left the bar.

"I know I said I wasn't looking for anything, but is there any chance of seeing you again?"

On his back, staring up at the ceiling, Zeke said, "No."

Leah nodded, and without saying good-bye, left the room.

Zeke remained on the bed, unmoving, as his mind relived the sex Sapphire and her lover had had.

"I hate you," he said softly. "I hate you."

The display on his cell phone lit up suddenly. He'd put it on the night table beside him. He reached over, picked it up, and looked at the screen.

Sapphire.

He put down the phone. The alcohol and sex had him tired. He closed his eyes and breathed slowly.

He fell asleep hoping that would be the last time she called.

Chapter 30

Jewell pulled into her parents' driveway, cut the engine, opened the car door quickly, doubled over, and dry heaved. She'd been fighting the nausea the whole way. Through her neighborhood and its silent, barely lit homes. On the highway, past broken-down cars in the grass in the median and cars pulled over by state troopers on the right. Past the vast homes with large windows and driveways large enough for Greyhound buses in her parents' development. She drove, her mouth watering, her stomach queasy. Somehow she managed to make it.

But now that she had . . .

Jewell gagged and dry heaved. She'd thrown up whatever food she'd had in her stomach already. Now all she had left was acid and phlegm. She dry heaved again and threw up nothing. She wanted to be in bed so badly, but something in the pit of her stomach, something other than the queasiness, was telling her that something was wrong.

She wiped her mouth with a napkin from her glove compartment. Ginger ale, bed, and darkness called. She grabbed her cell and called Sam again. She'd tried calling him, but he never answered and that worried her. Again she wondered about what it was that Sam said she had done. What had brought about such tension, anger, anxiety, and fear in his voice and eyes? What had she done that made him run out of the house? Made him ignore her calls?

What the fuck have you done?

Sam's words shook her, rocked her at her core. Something bad was happening, was going to happen, or had happened already.

Sam's voice mail picked up. "Sam . . . where are you? Why won't you pick up? Please call me back and tell me what's wrong. What did I do? Why did you run out the house like that? Sam . . . please call me back."

Jewell snapped her phone shut and slid it in her purse. She walked up to her parents' front door. Lights were on inside. Someone was home.

She rang the bell. Seconds went by without an answer. She rang the bell again and waited. Still no answer.

She grabbed her phone, called the house; nothing but the answering machine. She tried her mother's cell. When there was no answer, she tried her father's.

"Where are you?"

She peeked through the frosted glass on the side of the door, looking for any movement inside. She rang the bell again and knocked on the door.

"Mom! Dad!"

Something was wrong. She went through the keys on her keychain. Her father had given her a spare when they'd moved in. He wanted her to always know that she had somewhere to come home to. She'd never used the key before, never had to.

She rang the bell, knocked on the door again, and called out for her parents one last time. Same answer as before. She sighed and slid the key into the door.

Her hand shook and her heart beat heavily as she turned the doorknob and pushed the door open.

She stood at the threshold. "Hello? Mom? Dad?"

Silence responded.

She stepped into the marbled foyer, and closed the door behind her.

"Mom? Dad? Are you here?"

She walked slowly, softly, her body tense, and went to her father's study off to the right. She put her hand on the knob, and briefly thought of horror movies and the actors and actresses who always opened doors or went searching in darkness only to meet their untimely and gruesome demises. She'd always said that could never happen to her. That she'd wait for sunlight or for the lights to come on, or she would forego the search altogether.

But, of course, those were just movies. The actors had scripts to follow. The axes, machetes, butcher knives, pitchforks, and gloved hands with razor-sharp claws were all made of rubber or plastic. The blood they shed was ketchup or syrup. Their screams were rehearsed.

Jewell took a breath and wished she could forego pushing the door open, and wait for daylight to break, but she couldn't. She exhaled, opened the door, and pushed it open.

Darkness met her.

She walked inside slowly and reached for the light switch on the wall to the right of the door. She flipped the switch and her heart skipped a beat. "Dad?"

She looked around. Nothing but an empty, mahogany desk, bookshelves lined with books, and an empty leather loveseat with a lamp beside it, greeted her.

She took another breath, said, "Damn," and then stepped out of the room.

She called out for her parents again and continued to search through the lower level of the house, going to the kitchen next. From the kitchen she went to the sunroom, and then the family room, where lights had been left on. She grabbed her cell and made calls to Sam, her father, and mother again. All went unanswered.

She left no messages, closed her phone, went to the stairs, and ascended cautiously. *Not right*, she thought. *Something isn't right.*

Upstairs she went through the smaller bedrooms first, checking closets and under spare beds, before going to the master bedroom, only to have the same result. No one was home.

Jewell sat down on her parents' bed. Her stomach was twisting in knots again. Had started to when she was in the kitchen. She took a few deep breaths, trying to calm the ill feeling. When it finally subsided, she opened her cell to call Sam and her parents again, but before she could, she heard a noise coming from downstairs.

She stood up.

"Mom?"

She walked out of the bedroom and went to the stairs. She called out for her mother again. Silence still her only response. She thought about the horror movies again and then descended slowly,wishing for scripted scene.

When she reached the bottom of the staircase, she saw something that made her pause.

The front door was open.

She opened her cell, pressed the numbers 9-1-1, and was about to hit the talk button when someone appeared in the doorway.

Ty's other man, G. Dressed in all black. Black ski mask covering his face. Gun in his hand.

Jewell opened her mouth to scream, but before she could, G squeezed the trigger twice, sending two bullets ripping into Jewell's abdomen.

All of the air rushed from Jewell's lungs as she crumpled to the ground. Face down, she gasped as G hurried past her and ran up the stairs. His instructions were to make it look like a robbery. He went in search of jewelry and whatever other random items he could grab.

On the ground, Jewell tried to crawl to her cell phone, which lay several feet in front of her. She moved an inch, maybe two, and then lay still. She struggled to catch a breath as tears fell from her eyes. She tried to will herself to move again, but she couldn't, the pain too great.

She cried and felt her blood flow and pool beneath her. Her body felt warm from the blood, yet cold at the same time. Everything around her spun as she looked toward her cell phone through blurred vision.

Move.

That's all she had to do.

Move.

Reach out.

Grab it.

Call Sam.

He would answer this time.

Pain seared through her abdomen. Jewell cried. As she did, G came rushing down the stairs. He paused momentarily and looked down at her, and regretted not having his way with her before he'd shot her. She was sexy.

Damn shame someone wanted her dead. He shrugged, stomped down on her cell phone, shattering it, and then left quickly.

Jewell watched the soles of his shoes disappear through the door. "S . . . Sa . . . Sam . . ." she struggled.

Her eyes closed.

Then opened.

Then closed again.

She felt light.

"Sam . . ."

Pain seared through her belly again. She tried to take a deep breath but couldn't. She shivered, her blood beneath her no longer keeping her warm.

"Sam . . ."

Somewhere in the distance, she heard him call her name. It was far away at first, then closer.

Her eyes opened again as Sam's voice grew louder, almost sounding as though he were right beside her.

"S . . . Sa . . ."

Her eyes closed again.

Pain flooded through her body as she was suddenly manhandled like a rag doll.

"Jewell!"

It sounded like Sam's voice.

"Jewell! Oh God! No! No!"

Jewell opened her eyes. Her vision blurred, tear-filled and spotted, she looked at her husband.

"Jewell! Hold on, baby! Hold on!"

He cradled her and rocked her slowly.

"S . . . Sam . . ."

Sam held her tight. Kissed her on her forehead. "I'm right here, baby. I'm right here."

Jewell wanted to move. Wanted to reach up and caress his cheek. She couldn't. She whispered his name again.

"I'm right here," Sam said. "I'm right here."

Jewell shivered, took another look at her husband and then closed her eyes. As she faded into unconsciousness, she heard Sam on the phone, calling 9-1-1.

Chapter 31

"No! No, baby! No!"

Sam held Jewell in his arms tightly. He caressed her face. Kissed her forehead. Screamed her name again.

"No!"

He rocked her. Touched her cheek again. Her skin was clammy. She was sweating profusely. He kissed her on her forehead again, then her lips.

Blood.

There was so much blood.

Sam wiped tears from his eyes. Touched Jewell's face again. She was still alive. Barely. But still alive.

"Where the fuck is the ambulance!"

He clenched his jaws and pulled Jewell closer to him as though he could somehow keep her essence from sighing away.

"You're not going anywhere," he demanded. "Jewell, baby . . . you're not going anywhere! You're not leaving me. Do you hear me? You're not going to leave me!"

He kissed her lips, passed his hand through her hair, gritted his teeth, and looked up at the ceiling. He closed his eyes.

A few more minutes. Had he just gotten there a few minutes earlier. But the traffic. He'd been stuck in it on the highway. An SUV had run into a tractor-trailer, sending the trailer reeling over onto its side. The two right lanes had been completely shut down, forcing everyone to merge into one lane. He'd passed an alternate-route exit two exits prior, and the next one wasn't coming up until he'd passed the wreckage.

He'd been frantic on his phone, calling Zeke, calling Sapphire, trying anything short of calling the police to prevent tragedy from happening.

Tragedy.

"Oh God!"

Not Jewell. This wasn't supposed to happen. She wasn't supposed to have been there.

Sam has been stuck in the backup for more than forty-five minutes, cursing anyone who could be cursed. The driver of the SUV for being an irresponsible asshole behind the wheel, the driver of the tractor-trailer for not having any fucking reaction time—hadn't he heard of defensive driving? The police who couldn't make the traffic move fast enough, the firefighters who had no real purpose for being there, the ambulance for not getting the injured transported fast enough, the drivers in front of him for being too goddamned nosy and driving extra slow just hoping to get a glimpse of somebody or some body part sprawled on the ground, the people behind him for riding his fucking bumper—couldn't they see he couldn't go anywhere?

Sam cursed and cursed and cursed until he finally

passed the accident and was able to gun the engine, not giving a damn about the police troopers in the area.

Twenty minutes later, he was about to turn into Zeke and Sapphire's affluent development. His hope was that, despite the delay, he would somehow still make it in time to prevent something from happening. That hope was lost, however, when he passed G on the way in.

G was driving an inconspicuous, dark blue Honda Accord with tinted windows. Sam had seen him through the windshield. G had seen him, too. G making a right, Sam making a left, they'd passed one another in movie-like slow motion and locked eyes, slowing only momentarily.

Sam raced to Zeke's home, no longer hoping to prevent anything, but rather praying that Sapphire would still be alive. But when he saw Jewell's car in her parents' driveway, a terrifying chill came over him.

Sam cursed and kissed Jewell on her forehead again. "I'm so sorry, baby," he whispered. "I'm so sorry."

He cried, placed another gentle kiss on her forehead, cursed Zeke, cursed Sapphire, cursed the intern, cursed Ty, and cursed himself.

Had he just said no.

He would have been begging her for forgiveness, fighting for her love, insisting that the intern meant nothing, swearing that he only loved her, promising to never again betray her or the vows he'd taken.

Had he just said no.

He wouldn't be holding her with tears and blood flowing. He wouldn't be begging her to hold on, hold on. "Hold on, baby . . . please, hold on."

A siren screamed from outside.

Sam looked over his shoulder, saw flashing red and blue

lights. He turned back to Jewell. "The ambulance is here, baby. You're going to be OK."

He took hold of her hand and kissed it. He tried to force a smile, to reinforce and believe the words he'd spoken. That she was going to be all right. He tried to ignore the clamminess and the paling of her skin. He tried to ignore the fact that she didn't seem to be breathing.

His body began to shake as he cried harder. "Hold on, Jewell," he said, his throat constricted, his voice and spirit breaking. "Hold on."

Someone grabbed him by his shoulders. "Sir! Please back away!"

The EMTs. Two of them, a male and female.

They asked Sam to move again. He did and they immediately swarmed over Jewell.

"I don't have a pulse! Beginning chest compressions!"

On his knees, his shoulders slumped, Sam could only watch in horror as the scene unfolded. With every one to two–inch chest compression, Sam's body shook. With every two-second breath of air the EMT blew into Jewell's mouth, with every moment spent trying to save her life, Sam felt himself dying slowly.

"Oh my God! Jewell!"

Sam turned his head slowly and looked behind him. Sapphire was standing just inside the front door, her hands over her mouth.

"My baby! What happened to my baby!" She looked at Sam. "What happened to my baby!"

Sam tried to stand up and go to her, but he couldn't find the strength. He tried to speak, but he couldn't find his voice.

Sapphire called out for Jewell again and moved forward, demanding to know what had happened.

The female EMT told her that Jewell had been shot and that they were doing all they could to help her.

"Shot? Shot? You're giving her CPR? Why are you giving her CPR? Why are you pressing on her chest like that?"

"We're doing all we can, ma'am," the EMT said solemnly.

Sapphire knelt down in front of Sam and grabbed his shoulders. "What happened to my baby, Sam? What did you do to my baby?"

Sam stared at her.

He opened his mouth.

Sapphire shook him.

Called his name again.

Sam stared.

Blinked.

Heard nothing, but . . .

Time of death . . .

Sapphire let out a guttural scream, while Sam remained frozen, unable to move, barely able to breathe.

Sapphire screamed again. Asked God why.

Sam remained deathly still, seeing and hearing nothing, yet seeing and hearing it all at the same time.

Time of death . . .

Time of death . . .

Chapter 32

Sapphire was numb.

Her daughter was dead.

She sat, a statue of confusion, disbelief, grief, on her sofa.

Her daughter was dead.

That statement, hitting her in her chest, making it difficult to breathe, seemed incomprehensible. What did it mean exactly? It was like a whole other language. Greek, Arabic, Spanish, Chinese, French.

Dead?

A chill crept up her spine, wrapped itself around her shoulders, held her tightly. She shivered as tears fell down her face. "Why? Why did this have to happen?"

People moved around her. Forensics team, dusting for fingerprints, looking for clues.

No one answered her question.

She asked, "Why?" again and thought about her last conversation with her daughter. Jewell had known about

her and Tre. She'd paid to have photographs of them together. She'd made copies, sent a set to Tre, kept one for
herself, and sent a set to Zeke.

Just a few hours ago, Sapphire hated her daughter.
She'd been hurt, betrayed. Jewell had no idea what she'd
had to endure. The loneliness she'd been forced to accept.
The neglect. A few hours ago, she'd had hate in her heart
for her only child, and now her only child was gone.
Taken by someone who wanted nothing more than jewelry.

The police had gone through the house and told her
that her bedroom had been ransacked and her jewelry
taken. Jewell must have surprised the person or persons,
and so they'd shot her and ran. The police promised to do
all they could to find out who the person or persons were.
They left Sapphire on the couch, and then went outside to
talk to Sam.

Sapphire cried, and with her hands trembling, tried to
call Zeke again. She'd been trying to reach him since after
she'd last spoken to Jewell. Jewell had confirmed it with
her confession, but Sapphire knew the last time they'd
had sex that he'd known.

His daughter was dead.

Sapphire broke down, dropped her cell after another
unsuccessful attempt at reaching her husband, and buried
her face in her hands.

Not my daughter, she thought. *Not my daughter.*

She cried, while the forensics team did their job without so much as a second glance in her direction. Being in
the presence of grief was nothing new to them.

Sapphire cried and shook as questions ran through her
mind.

Why did this have to happen? Why had Jewell been

there? Had she come to apologize? To chastise her
mother even more? Had she come looking for her father
to make sure he knew the truth? What if she had never
gone to see Tre? Could she have prevented her daughter's
death or would she have been killed, too? Why had Sam
been here? How did he know Jewell would be here? Had
Jewell called him?

Sapphire cried hard tears as the CSI team finished their
jobs and left her alone.

"My fault," she whispered. "This is my fault."

Without the arrangement with Tre, none of this would
have happened. Jewell wouldn't have caught her. Pictures
wouldn't have been taken. Pictures wouldn't have been
sent. Zeke wouldn't have left. Jewell wouldn't have been
there. Jewell wouldn't have died.

She furiously wiped an unending stream of tears away
from her eyes. "My fault," she said again. "It's all my fault,
Sam."

He'd just walked into the living room. Sapphire looked
at him as he stood, stoic, leaning against the far wall, his
arms folded across his chest.

"Why did this happen, Sam? Why did my baby die? Why
did this have to happen? Why did God do this? Why, Sam?
Why now?" She'd wanted to fix her relationship with Jewell. She'd wanted them to be closer. "Why, Sam?"

She looked at him, begging him with her eyes to provide answers that she desperately needed.

Sam looked back at her, but didn't speak.

Sapphire wiped tears, sniffled. "Sam?" His silence worried her. His glare back even more so. There was something in his eyes. Her tears continued to fall as she watched
him watching her, his jaw tight, his eyes getting darker.
"She . . . she told you, didn't she?"

She could tell by the way he'd been staring at her. There was an underlying anger beneath the pain, beneath the grief. He could tell her that he didn't know, but she knew he'd be lying.

Sam continued to stare at her silently, his jaw getting tighter, his nostrils widening.

"How long?" Sapphire asked. "How long have you known?"

Sam stared. Remained mute.

Sapphire shook her head slowly. "I . . . I never meant . . ." She paused, drew a short breath. "I never meant . . ." She paused again and buried her face in her hands. "It should have been me," she said, her voiced muffled by the palms of her hands. "Oh God. It should have been me."

Cold, hard, stinging tears of guilt and remorse fell down her face. "It should have been me," she said again.

"Where were you?" Sam asked suddenly, his voice low, his tone flat.

Sapphire pulled her hands away from her face and looked up at him. "What?"

Sam dropped his arms to his sides and balled his hands into tight fists. "Where the fuck were you?" he asked again.

"Sam . . . what—"

"Those bullets . . ." Sam paused and gritted his teeth. "Those bullets were meant for you."

Sapphire looked at him, confusion in her eyes. "What did you say?"

"Those bullets were meant for you, Sapphire."

Sapphire shook her head. "What . . . what do you mean, Sam? Meant for me?"

"Jewell wasn't supposed to be here. You were. Where the fuck were you?" he yelled out, making Sapphire jump.

"What are you saying?"

"It was one guy," Sam said. "And he took the jewelry to make it look like a robbery."

"Sam?"

"You were supposed to be here. Alone. Jewell was supposed to be home."

"No, Sam," Sapphire said as shock and disbelief rifled through her.

"He was supposed to come while you were here. He was supposed to shoot you and then take the jewelry and whatever else he could find and leave. I was supposed to call Zeke and tell him when he could come to discover your body. Why the fuck weren't you here?"

"No," Sapphire said, rising from the couch. She went to him.

"Zeke saw the pictures, Sapphire, and he wanted you dead."

"No, Sam. Please . . . No!" She was standing in front of him now. She grabbed his hand.

He pulled it away. "Zeke found me cheating on Jewell. I was supposed to make your death happen. That was what I had to do to keep him from taking everything away from me."

Sapphire reached out for him again. "No . . . no, Sam!"

He pushed her back, sending her to the ground. "You're supposed to be fucking dead! Not Jewell!"

"No! No! No!"

Chapter 33

Sam wanted to rush forward and grab Sapphire by her throat. He wanted to choke her until she couldn't breathe. She was supposed to be dead.

He closed his eyes tightly.

Pressed the palms of his hands against his temples.

Tried to squeeze away the tumultuous anger, regret, pain, guilt, and hatred, all clamoring together to form an orchestral sound that was driving him slowly insane.

He opened his eyes and glared at Sapphire.

She was crying, yelling, "No! No!"

"Jewell should have been home!" Sam screamed.

He wanted so badly to hurt her. He wanted to kick her down and punch her, each blow representing retaliation for everything that had happened. For Sapphire's infidelity. For God allowing Jewell to discover the affair.

Retaliation.

For the pictures taken and sent. For Zeke and his damned ultimatum.

Retaliation.

For his own infidelity. For giving in to Zeke's demand. For contacting Ty. For giving him an address only, and not a picture of Sapphire.

Sam squeezed his eyes tightly again as Sapphire's words rang in his ears.

It was all her fault.

He shook his head. Sapphire's words—they were only partly true. She was at fault, yes, but he was too. Jewell wouldn't have died if he'd only been man enough to deal with the consequences of his actions.

Jewell died in his arms.

Her blood would forever be on his hands.

On all of their hands.

He looked down at Sapphire. No longer screaming, she sat on the ground, her arms pinning her knees against her chest. She was crying and rocking back and forth slowly.

She'd betrayed Zeke.

Sam had betrayed Jewell.

He wanted to hate her, but he couldn't. "Sapphire."

She raised her head slowly.

"It's my fault too," Sam said solemnly. "I . . . I cheated on Jewell and Zeke found out. Jewell is . . . is . . ." He paused as tears fell slowly from the corners of his eyes. "She's gone because of me."

Sapphire's bottom lip quivered as a fresh wave of tears flooded from her eyes. She stood up and wrapped her arms around him and buried her face into the middle of his chest and cried with him.

She'd lost a daughter.

He'd lost a wife.

They would forever be bonded by actions that would haunt them for the rest of their days.

Sam held her tightly until his cell phone rang from inside of his pocket.

He and Sapphire looked at one another. Sapphire backed away and wrapped herself up in her own arms. Sam reached into his pocket and pulled out his cell. He looked at the display, then at Sapphire as she watched him intensely. He nodded.

It was Zeke.

He raised the cell to his ear.

Was about to hit the talk button when Sapphire said, "Tell him he can come home now."

Sam looked at her.

She looked at Sam.

"Tell him," Sapphire said again.

Sam kept his lips tight and with his eyes on Sapphire, connected the call.

Chapter 34

Sapphire hadn't stopped calling him. He'd waited for the calls to stop. Waited for Sam to call him to tell him that it was all over. That his wife was dead. That he could go home. He'd waited, but the calls just wouldn't stop.

Why?

What happened?

Had things gone awry?

Had Sam backed out?

Why the hell did she keep calling?

He didn't want to call, but he couldn't take it anymore. His patience had worn thin and he needed to know why things hadn't happened.

"She's still calling me. Why?"

He hadn't even given Sam a chance to speak.

On the other end of the call, Sam said, "You can come home now."

Zeke's heart skipped and then beat heavily. "What did you say?"

"You can come home."

"It's done?"

"It's done."

Zeke stared at his reflection in the mirror across from him. He was still in his hotel room, sitting on the bed.

His wife was dead.

His reflection smiled at him.

"And the headless man?"

"It's done," Sam said again.

"Do you have confirmation?"

"I do."

"And my wife is dead?"

Sam exhaled heavily. "Yes." His voice was low, subdued. He had the sound of death on his voice. There was no doubt in Zeke's mind; his wife was dead. He could go home. He could start life anew.

"There's no turning back now, Sam. You know that, right? Your hand is as red as mine."

"I . . . I know," Sam said, his voice taut.

"We have roles to play now, Sam. I hope you can handle yours."

There was a slight pause before Sam said, "OK."

"Sam?"

"Yes, Zeke?"

"Where's Jewell?"

Nothing but silence answered him.

"Sam?" Zeke called.

Still nothing but silence. He pulled the cell away from his ear and looked at it. The call was still connected. He put it back to his ear. "Sam?"

Silence and then sniffling.

"What's wrong, Sam?"

Sam cleared his throat. "N—nothing."

"You don't sound like nothing's wrong."

"Ev—everything is . . ." Sam paused for several seconds and then spoke again. "Everything's fine, Zeke."

"Where's Jewell, Sam?"

Zeke waited as Sam took a deep breath and exhaled heavily. "She . . . she's sleeping."

Zeke closed his eyes a bit. The tone in Sam's voice—something about it made him uneasy. "Is she OK? She called me a few times earlier, but I didn't want to talk to her until everything was done."

"She . . . she's fine," Sam replied, his voice fading.

"She's going to need you, Sam. My daughter's going to need your support to help her through this."

Sam didn't respond.

"You're going to have to handle it, Sam. You're going to have to keep it together."

Barely audible, Sam said, "I . . . I need to go, Zeke."

Sam ended the call before Zeke could say another word.

Zeke looked at his reflection in the mirror. Sapphire's death had hit Sam hard. His tone had been grief-filled and laced with guilt. He would have to have a talk with him. He would have to reinforce the need to keep himself together.

His wife was dead.

Funny, he thought. He'd expected that fact to hit him in the way it hit Sam. His wife, the woman he'd loved at one time more than anything in the world.

He felt nothing.

No sadness. No remorse. No regret. He would never see or hear her again. He would never feel her warmth. Only in his memories would that be possible.

Zeke took a breath and thought about Sapphire being

gone. He sat still. Gone. Dead. He digested the two words. He sat still. Waited for it to hit him. The emotional turmoil.

He sat still.

Breathed.

Waited.

He felt nothing.

He rose from the bed. He had two more roles to play before it would all be over: the grieving widower and the grieving father.

He and his reflection shared a lingering glance, admiration in their eyes.

He would go home and play the roles. And if Sam couldn't perform his, then he would have to meet a fate the same as Sapphire's. It was a brand new life, and no one was going to get in the way of his happiness. He got dressed and prepared to go home.

Chapter 35

"**I**s he coming?"

Sapphire looked at Sam, her heart beating heavily.

Her husband. The man she'd given her heart to and shared vows with. The man to whom she'd given up her body. The man to whom she'd given her soul. Her husband of thirty-four years. He'd wanted her dead.

He'd been somewhere waiting for a call letting him know that he could come home. That his wife's lifeless, cold, stiff body was waiting to be found.

He would put on an act, feign shock and grief. He would shed tears. He'd have a viewing and then a funeral. Would probably have a hundred or so attendees. He'd be pitied for his loss. People would offer their condolences. Tell him that if he needed anything at all, not to hesitate to call and let them know. They would be there to help see him through the rough time.

Zeke would thank them for their kindness and their gratitude with hugs and smiles and tears. He'd tell them that he appreciated their support. That it meant a lot knowing he had friends like them to lean on. He would cry some more in front of them.

All for the woman he'd had killed.

At least that was his plan.

Sam said, "Yes."

Sapphire nodded. "My daughter is dead, Sam. My daughter, your wife. Zeke killed her. You had a hand in it, too."

Sam kept his jaw tight and didn't say anything.

"Why did you cheat on Jewell?"

Sam blinked several times, swallowed, dropped his chin to his chest, and looked down at the hardwood floor. He breathed slowly, deeply. "I . . . I was being selfish," he said, his voice just above a whisper.

"Did Jewell satisfy you?"

Choking back tears, Sam nodded. "Jewell is . . ." he said, grimaced in pain, and continued, "was . . . perfect. I couldn't have asked for a better woman, a better wife."

"Was it an affair?"

He shook his head. "No. She meant nothing to me. It happened only one time. One fucking time." Sam's chest rose and fell as he took a deep breath, trying to keep his composure.

Sapphire frowned. "Zeke is . . . was a good man, but he has an obsessive-compulsive nature about him. When something grabs his interest, he throws himself into it completely, and when he does, he becomes neglectful. Zeke threw himself into building the company. In doing so, he forgot about his wife. Of course, I knew that for the first few years, his attention and time were going to be fixed on trying to make things happen. I understood and accepted that. But I also expected that after things were up and running, even though he couldn't pull himself away from it completely, he would start to put some focus back on me. Not much of course, but at least enough to let me know that I was still desired, still cherished. That I was still relevant and necessary as a wife, lover, and friend.

"My relationship with Tre . . . it wasn't an affair. He was a gigolo and I paid him to satisfy me. I was lonely, Sam. Lonely and I needed companionship. I needed to feel like a woman. Every woman needs that. We get older, we have kids, and our bodies change. Our breasts sag, our hips spread, the bulge around our stomachs grow. Real women need to feel desired. I felt like a twenty-something with Tre. I felt wanted. It didn't matter that I paid for it."

Sapphire took a breath and exhaled slowly.

"You were wrong for cheating on Jewell. Neglectful or not, I was wrong for cheating on Zeke. But . . ." She paused again, stepped toward Sam, and put her hand beneath his chin and lifted it, forcing him to look her in the eye. "What we did was just cheating, Sam. It wasn't a terrorist act. It was cheating. You and I, Zeke, and even Jewell . . . we're all imperfect. We all make mistakes. Yes, we had a hand in Jewell's death, but things should have never gotten this far. Zeke judged us as though he were perfect. Jewell is dead because Zeke acted as though he were the perfect man, the perfect husband.

"Jewell and I didn't have the greatest relationship, but she was my daughter. We had time to fix things between us and grow closer, and I think we would have. Jewell is dead, Sam. Two wrongs don't make a right, but I want Zeke to pay. I hate him for what he did, and I want him to pay." She paused again and gave Sam an intense, serious gaze. "You're going to have to pay, too."

Sam inhaled, then exhaled. "I can't possibly pay any more than I already have," he said.

Sapphire gave an acknowledging nod. "I know, despite your mistake, you loved Jewell with all your heart."

Tears fell from Sam's eyes as he nodded. "I'm sorry," he said. "I never wanted any of this to happen."

"We're all sorry, Sam."

Sam turned and walked slowly out of the family room and the house, leaving Sapphire alone. Zeke was coming home to be surprised and devastated all at the same time.

Chapter 36

*What goes around comes around.
Karma.*

Sam thought he'd outrun his past and all of the things he'd done, but the circle of karma in his life hadn't been completed until now, with Jewell's death. Karma had finally completed its revolution and was now sitting on his lap.

Sapphire had said he had to pay. He said he couldn't have paid any more. He'd been wrong.

He drove down the highway to his old neighborhood with revenge, remorse, and repentance in his heart and on his mind. He grabbed his cell and dialed Ty's number.

The "Pop Champagne" ring tone blasted in his ear momentarily before Ty answered. "I hope you're callin' me to tell me you got the rest of my money, nigga."

Sam clenched his jaws. "I'll be at Old Man Hop's in fifteen minutes." He ended the call, tossed his cell to the passenger side floorboard, tightened his grip around the steering wheel, and focused back on the road.

Fifteen minutes later he was pulling into Old Man Hop's chop shop.

He cut the engine as Ty stood beside Loc'. G, who had raised the gate, allowing Sam to drive in, now lowered the gate and remained behind the car. Sam looked at G in the rear view mirror and thought about the last time he'd laid eyes on him. Jewell had been dying then.

Sam took a breath as Sapphire's words ran through his mind.

He had to pay.

For all that had happened. For his inability to say no to Zeke. For hiring Ty and his boys. He had to pay.

He exhaled and stepped out of the car and closed the door.

Ty said, "I don't see no briefcase in your hand, nigga."

Sam looked down at the concrete floor. It was stained with oil and tire treads. Pretty soon it would be stained with something else. He took another deep breath and let it out slowly. His heart beat was surprisingly calm, his nerves steady, and the palms of his hands cool and dry. He took one final deep breath, savored the feel and pressure in his lungs being full, and then looked up at Ty. He shook his head. "There's no briefcase," he said evenly.

Ty looked at Loc', who shrugged his shoulders. Ty looked back to Sam. "What you mean there's no brief-case?"

"I mean I'm not paying you any more money."

Ty's expression became dark. "What you mean you ain't payin' me? Nigga, was you smokin' on your way here?"

"Your boy . . ." Sam turned his head and looked at G who was still standing by the gate. "You killed the wrong person!"

G looked at him skeptically. "What do you mean I killed

the wrong person? I killed whoever you said was gonna be in the fuckin' house, dude."

"You were supposed to kill my mother-in-law. Not my fuckin' wife, nigga!" Sam turned back to Ty. "My wife is dead, Ty. I got no more money for you!"

Ty pulled out a 9 m. "What the fuck? Nigga, you came here to die or what? I don't give a fuck which one of your bitches died. You paid to have a job done. You gave instructions on how it was supposed to be done, and those instructions were followed."

"He shot my fucking wife!" Sam screamed. His heart was beating heavily now as adrenaline kicked into high gear.

"Nigga, I told you I don't give a fuck. You said the bitch would be alone in the house. Now, I'm gonna give you one more chance, and that's only because we used to be boys. Get me my motherfuckin' money or shit's gonna get real ugly for you."

Ty held the gun strong and firm. Loc' stood beside him with his pistol drawn, too. Sam was sure G had his gun out as well.

Sam stared at Ty, who glared back at him with the eyes and body language of a bull about to charge. He hadn't been the gunman, but he had to pay too. Sapphire's words whispered in his head again.

His heart pounded. Felt as though it were trapped inside of his chest and was determined to break free. His breathing quickened. Time slowed to a crawl.

In his arms, blood leaking from her wounds, his wife had taken her last breath. Sam would always remember that. He'd always have the image of the look of shock, fear, and pain on her face as she looked up at him.

He couldn't handle that. Day after day, that image would

haunt him. He wasn't strong enough. He wasn't man enough to pay for his cowardice. He just couldn't.

In his waist band he'd concealed a .22. Zeke had given it to him. Said to keep it on him just in case he met a "Sam" of his own that he couldn't convince to go and eat Italian food. He'd kept it in the glove compartment, and just before he reached the shop, he removed it and tucked it behind his belt.

Time froze.

Sound disappeared.

Sam pulled the .22 free. For a split second, he thought about shooting Ty, but then turned and faced G. He'd shot Jewell. He'd killed his wife. It wasn't his fault, but he had to die first. If he got the chance, he'd kill Ty next.

He squeezed the trigger. Once, twice, three times.

G grunted and fell back as bullets hit him in his chest and midsection.

Seconds later, bullets ripped through Sam's shoulders and back, some exiting through his chest. He fell to the ground, his upper torso burning, bleeding. He crawled until someone kicked him repeatedly in his ribs, forcing him to roll over onto his back.

Sam looked up.

Ty stood above him, the muzzle of his 9 m aimed at Sam's head. "Stupid motherfucker," he said, and then squeezed the trigger.

Just before the bullet made impact with his forehead, Sam smiled.

The last thing he would see would be Ty standing above him.

Sam smiled.

Chapter 37

Zeke pulled up to his house. It was three o'clock in the morning. A full moon shone in the dark, early morning sky. All of the lights in the house were off. The moon cast an eerie glow over the house.

Zeke cut the engine and stared at his home. In a few seconds he would walk in and discover his wife's dead body. He'd worked on his frantic 9-1-1 phone call on the drive home.

H—help! My . . . my wife . . . she . . . Someone sh— shot my wife! Oh God!

He'd pretty much perfected it. The inflection in the rise and pitch, the perfect levels of paranoia, fear, disbelief, and grief. He would deserve an Oscar for his performance.

He opened his car door and stepped out. His steps were light and casual as he made his way to the house. At the front door he paused and looked up at the moon, looking for the face in it. He found it and gave it a wink, and then opened his door, flicked the light in the foyer, and stepped inside.

He closed the door behind him and stood still in the silence.

"Honey, I'm home!"

He waited for a response and smiled.

He moved away from the door, went to his study, and turned on the light. "Where are you, baby? Where they leave you, you bitch!"

The study empty, he moved away and went to the kitchen, turned on the lights there, saw nothing, and moved on to the sunroom and then the family room. "Where are you, bitch! Where did you take your last breath?"

He left the family room and went to the staircase. He paused and looked down. The maroon tile beneath his foot was a little sticky.

He stepped off of the tile and made his way up the stairs. "Where are you darling?" He chuckled. Darling. He never used that word. "Honey? Darling?"

He was halfway up the staircase now.

"Are you in the bedroom, honey? It's fitting that you'd be there, you fucking whore!"

"I'm not in the bedroom."

Zeke stopped moving.

That voice. Coming from the top of the staircase. It was frighteningly familiar.

He looked up.

The light at the top of the staircase came on.

Sapphire. His wife. Staring down at him.

"Wh—What . . ."

"You fucking asshole!" Sapphire shrieked. "You fucking bastard!"

Zeke leaned against the banister as his knees grew

weak. He shook his head. "It . . . it's not possible. You're . . . You're . . ."

"What, Zeke?" Sapphire yelled. "I'm what?"

"You're . . . you're supposed to be dead?"

"Jewell is the one who's dead!"

"Wh . . . what?"

Tears erupting from her eyes, Sapphire screamed, "I wasn't here! Jewell was. She was looking for you, you piece of shit! The guy you hired thought she was me! He shot her! She's dead. You killed our daughter!"

Zeke's chest hurt and burned as he struggled to breath, struggled to deal with Sapphire's existence above him, struggled to comprehend what she'd said. Everything around him spun and became unfocused. He began to shake.

Jewell.

Dead?

He shook his head. "You're . . . you're lying! You're fucking lying!"

"Your daughter died at the bottom of the steps!" Sapphire raged. "You killed her, Zeke! You killed my baby!"

The bottom of the steps. The stickiness.

Zeke shook his head again. "No . . . No!" He put his hand to his chest. He felt as though he were having a heart attack. His daughter? It couldn't be. He shook his head yet again. "You're lying! I . . . I spoke to Sam. He said you were dead. He said Jewell was fine!"

"I told him to say that, Zeke. I was standing beside him when he told you you could come home. I was standing right there when you called to confirm that I was dead, you piece of shit!"

Zeke couldn't breathe. He could barely think. His daughter. No. Not his daughter. Not Jewell. Not his princess.

He took a step. "You're lying!" he insisted again.

"You, bastard! Your plan backfired. Our daughter is dead!"

Another step up, Zeke insisted again, "You're lying!"

"Jewell sent you the pictures, Zeke. She sent you those goddamned pictures!"

Zeke knotted his head in frustration. "What? What do you mean she sent me the pictures?"

"She found out about me, and she hated me for it. She hired a professional photographer and had the pictures taken and then sent you the photos."

Zeke shook his head. Jewell had sent him the photos. "She sent the photos?" he said, his voice growing soft with disbelief.

"She wanted you to confront me, Zeke! She wanted you to take those photographs and throw them in my face. But you couldn't do that, could you? Your pride just wouldn't let you come and confront me. And you know what, you fucking bastard? It wasn't even a goddamned affair! I was paying to be fucked because I was lonely! You neglected me, Zeke. You put work and everything else before me, before us, time and time again. This . . . this is your fault! You pushed me into another man's arms, Zeke!"

Zeke stumbled and fell against the banister as his legs gave out. He took rapid breaths, felt as though he were hyperventilating. Confusion, angst, and dread funneled around him, forming the most horrific tornado.

The pictures, sent by Jewell.

Sapphire, his wife, with another man.

Sam with the intern.

Sapphire alive.

Jewell dead.

The tornado swirled. Knocked him back. Knocked him sideways. Almost picked him up and threw him down.

He put his hand over his mouth, shook his head, squeezed his cheeks with his thumb and middle finger.

Jewell had been calling him over and over and now she was dead.

The tornado spun.

"You're supposed to be dead!" he screamed as tears fell from his eyes. "You're supposed to be dead, you whore!"

"The police are on the way, asshole! I called them. I'm going to give them this when they come!" She held up a micro-cassette recorder. "You're going to get life, you son of a bitch! I've been recording you from the moment you walked inside! I have you, Zeke! I have you!"

Zeke couldn't breathe, couldn't think, the tornado sucking away all of the oxygen, leaving his mind in disarray.

Jewell . . . dead.

Sapphire . . . alive.

It wasn't supposed to be this way.

Above the tumultuous confusion in his head, Zeke heard sirens. Approaching the house. Coming to take him to jail.

But he wasn't a criminal. Sapphire was. Her betrayal, her deceit—that was the real crime. He wasn't to blame. He couldn't be. He couldn't and wouldn't do anything to hurt his little girl, his little princess.

He wasn't to blame.

He shook his head again as the wail of the police sirens grew louder. He looked up at Sapphire. Her crime . . . Her crime.

"You bitch!" he screamed. "I'm going to kill you!"

He charged up the remaining stairs toward Sapphire. He'd imagined doing it many times over, but this time it would be real. He was going to choke her. She was going to die like she was supposed to.

He raced up to the top.

Sapphire screamed and then removed a baseball bat she'd had hidden at her side.

Zeke had kept the bat at his bedside for protection. He had a gun, too, but he'd never told her where he kept it.

Sapphire screamed and swung out.

Zeke never saw the blow coming, but felt it crash against his temple.

The tornado finally managed to pick him up and throw him down.

Zeke tumbled and twisted backward and sideways at forty-five, thirty-six, and fifty-four-degree angles down the steps, until he hit the bottom, his neck and back broken.

He stared up at the ceiling through blurred, spotted vision. He was in pain, feeling himself slowly fading.

He wheezed. His insides burned. He felt blood running from where the bat had connected.

His daughter was dead.

He was lying where she'd taken her last breath.

He would be dead soon.

Sapphire would still be alive.

He wanted to cry, to scream, to laugh, but he could only lay involuntarily still.

Sirens screamed from outside of the door.

Zeke closed his eyes and went to a place where Jewell would never know death, and he and Sapphire would always exist with promises to live faithfully as one.

Epilogue

Zeke hadn't died.

Sapphire thought he had.

As she stood at the top of the staircase staring down at him with the micro-cassette recorder in one hand and the baseball bat in the other, she thought for sure that he'd gone down where the temperature made your flesh blister and pop open, where a man dressed in red tights with horns on his head and a pitchfork in his hand stood with a fanged smile.

But he hadn't.

The police stormed into the house, found Zeke unmoving at the bottom of the staircase, his eyes closed, and announced that he still had a pulse. Several minutes later, the paramedics were taking Zeke away on a stretcher to the hospital, while police officers listened to the recording on the micro-cassette tape. When the tape was shut off, condolences were given for the events that had taken place, and Sapphire was left alone. She'd defended herself. There wasn't any more that needed to be said.

Five days later, Sapphire sat with a newspaper in her hand, sitting beside Zeke, who lay in a hospital bed paralyzed from the neck down. Sapphire sighed. She didn't know why she was there. Zeke wanted her dead, and had tried his best to kill her, but there she was, back for a fourth visit.

"I buried our daughter and son-in-law today," she said. "Their bodies are lying side by side. They have a beautiful headstone made of granite, with the inscription 'beloved daughter and beloved son.'"

This was the first time she'd spoken to him. She hadn't been able to bring herself to speak before this.

She took a breath and flipped through the pages and came to a stop on page three. In the middle, off to the right, there was an article about Tre. He'd been found dead in his apartment with multiple stab wounds to his stomach and chest. The police were calling it a robbery, as his Xbox 360, flat-screen plasma television, iPod, and several other random items had been stolen.

Sapphire thought about Tre and sadness fell over her soul. Collateral damage, that's what he'd been. Collateral damage in a war between husband and wife. Sapphire wiped a tear away from the corner of her eye. Tre's death was on her shoulders and no one else's. It would forever weigh down on her conscience. She looked over at Zeke. "You should be dead," she said evenly.

She folded the newspaper in half and slid it in her purse, and then rose from her chair and stood over Zeke. She looked him in his eyes intensely as he stared back at her, his eyeballs the only thing able to move.

Her mind went back to the funeral, back to the moment

when the caskets had been lowered into the earth. Emotions tugged at her from every possible angle. Sadness, pain, grief, anger, hatred, remorse, fear. Overwhelmed, she'd dropped down to her knees and remained there, refusing to let anyone help her up. The grief extreme, she had stayed on the ground, sobbing heavily. She'd been alone for a half hour before she finally found strength enough to get up.

She stared down at her husband.

She said, "Their child's empty casket is lying between them, Zeke."

She paused to let her words sink in. Zeke looked at her, his eyes widening.

"Jewell was six weeks pregnant. They discovered that when they did the autopsy."

Sapphire stared as Zeke's breathing quickened. He moaned slightly, unable to speak because of the breathing tube in his throat. His eyes opened more and began to well with tears.

"The inscription on our grandchild's headstone reads 'To our beloved Grandchild. Taken far too soon. Watch over us, little angel. Watch over us.' We'll never get to be grandparents, Ezekiel. We will never know that joy."

Zeke moaned again. Sapphire could see in his eyes that he was trying to move. She looked up. The beeping on his heart monitor had increased. She looked down at him.

"Your daughter, your son-in-law, your grandchild . . . all dead, Zeke. Dead because of you. Because of your pride, your ego. You have to live with that. And . . . so do I." She wrapped herself up in her arms, the admittance of her own hand in what had occurred making her cold.

Heart rate increasing, tears falling down from the corner of his eyes and resting on his pillow, Zeke moaned again.

"Remember what you've done when you're in hell, Zeke. Remember what you've done."

Sapphire looked up at the monitor, and then back down at him. His eyes began to roll into the back of his head. His body began to shake. Sapphire stared and thought about being at the top of the staircase.

"You should be dead, Zeke," she whispered. She bent forward, gave him a kiss on his forehead, and turned away from him. As she did, nurses and doctors came rushing into the room, frantically trying to stop his seizure.

Sapphire walked out of the room.

She thought he'd died before.

This time, she was sure he would.

One hour later, Sapphire was looking up at the sun through a pair of shades. It had been a while since she'd taken time to appreciate the sun and the light and warmth it provided.

She'd received a call twenty minutes after leaving the hospital.

Zeke was dead.

Sapphire took a breath as the sun's rays washed over her, and looked toward the house she used to call home. A "sold" sign hung in the front yard. After all that had happened, remaining there had just been impossible. There was too much pain, too much death injected into its walls. Selling it had been a necessity on Sapphire's long road to recovery.

"They seem like a really great family."

Sapphire turned and looked at her realtor, Nancy. She gave a half smile. "Yes, they do."

She turned and looked back to the family as they walked into the house. Mommy, daddy, and their little girl. Sapphire closed her eyes and prayed for them to be unaffected by the ghosts they'd left behind. She opened her eyes and turned back to Nancy. "So the condo will be ready in two days?"

Nancy nodded. "Yes."

"Good."

Nancy got into her BMW and drove off.

Sapphire stood still for a long moment and looked at the house one last time, then got into her car and drove away alone. Something she would forever be.

Book Club
Discussion Questions

1. Who do you think was the catalyst for the events that took place in the book?

2. Were you surprised by Zeke's emotional breakdown?

3. Could you sympathize with Sam's decision to go along with Zeke?

4. Was Jewell wrong for sending the pictures?

5. If in Jewell's position, would you have confronted Sapphire?

6. Do you think Zeke was truly hurt by Sapphire's infidelity, or had his ego/pride just been bruised?

7. How did you feel at the end?

8. Do you think Zeke would have changed his ways had Sapphire communicated with him initially about her feelings?

9. Would Sam and Jewell's marriage have survived had Sam confessed about his infidelity?

10. Who was the true victim in this tale?